THE MAGIC WALKING STICK

" Magic," gasped the dull of mind,
  When the harnessed earth and skies
Drew the nomads of their kind
  To uncharted emperies—
Whispers round the globe were sped,
  Construed was the planets' song.

But the little boy playing in the orchard said,
Conning his tale in the orchard said,
  " *I knew it all along.*"

Power deduced from powerless dust,
  Nurture from the infertile grave ;
Much the years may hold in trust,
  Space a thrall and Time a slave.
Hark the boasting of the wise :
  " First are we of those that know ! "

But the little boy playing by the roadside cries,
Trundling his hoop by the roadside cries,
  " *I said it long ago.*"

THE MAGIC
WALKING STICK

John Buchan

Illustrated by
Morton Sale

CANONGATE · KELPIES

First published 1932 by Hodder & Stoughton Limited, London
First published in Kelpies 1985
Second impression 1989

Copyright © the Executors of Lord Tweedsmuir's Will Trust

Cover illustration by Jill Downie

Printed in Great Britain
by Cox & Wyman Ltd, Reading, Berkshire

ISBN 0 86241 097 5

*The publishers acknowledge the financial assistance
of the Scottish Arts Council in the
publication of this volume*

to
Carola, Margaret, and Jeremy

CANONGATE PUBLISHING LTD
17 JEFFREY STREET, EDINBURGH EH1 1DR

CONTENTS

CONTENTS

CHAPTER ONE

THE COMING OF THE STAFF

WHEN Bill came back for long-leave that autumn half, he had before him a complicated programme of entertainment. Thomas, the keeper, whom he revered more than anyone else in the world, was to take him in the afternoon to try for a duck in the big marsh called Alemoor. In the evening Hallowe'en was to be celebrated in the nursery with his small brother Peter, and he was to be permitted to come down to dinner, and to sit up afterwards until ten o'clock. Next day, which was Sunday, would be devoted to wandering about with Peter, hearing from him all the appetising home news, and pouring into his greedy ears the gossip of the foreign world of school. On Monday morning, after a walk with the dogs, he was to motor to London, lunch with Aunt Alice, and then, after a noble tea, return to school in time for lock-up.

This seemed to Bill to be all that could be desired in the way of excitement. But he did not know just how exciting that long-leave was destined to be.

The first shadow of a cloud appeared after luncheon, when he had changed into knicker-bockers and Thomas and the dogs were waiting by the gun-room door. Bill could not find his own proper stick. It was a long hazel staff, given him by the second stalker at Glenmore the year before—a staff rather taller than Bill, a glossy hazel, with a shapely polished crook, and without a ferrule, like all good stalking-sticks.

He hunted for it high and low, but it could not be found. Without it in his hand Bill felt that the expedition lacked something vital, and he was not prepared to take instead one of his father's shooting-sticks, as Groves, the butler, recommended. Nor would he accept a knobbly cane proffered by Peter. Feeling a little aggrieved and imperfectly equipped, he rushed out to join Thomas. He would cut himself an ashplant in the first hedge.

In the first half-mile he met two magpies, and this should have told him that something was going to happen. It is right to take off your cap to a single magpie, or to three, or to five, but never to an even number, for an even number means mischief. But Bill, looking out for ashplants, was heedless, and had uncovered his head before he remembered the rule.

Then, as he and Thomas ambled down the lane which led to Alemoor, they came upon an old man sitting under a hornbeam.

This was the second warning, for of course a hornbeam is a mysterious tree. Moreover, though there were hornbeams in Bill's garden, they did not flourish elsewhere in that country-side. Had Bill been on his guard he would have realised that the hornbeam had no business there, and that he had never seen it before. But there it was, growing in a grassy patch by the side of the lane, and under it sat an old man.

He was a funny little wizened old man, in a shabby long green overcoat which had once been black ; and he wore on his head the oldest and tallest and greenest bowler hat that ever graced a human head. It was quite as tall as the topper which Bill wore at school. Thomas, who had a sharp eye for poachers and vagabonds, did not stop to question him, but walked on as if he did not see him—which should have warned Bill that something queer was afoot. Also Gyp, the spaniel, and Shawn, the Irish setter, at the sight of him dropped their tails

between their legs and remembered an engagement a long way off.

But Bill stopped, for he saw that the old man
had a bundle under his arm, a bundle of ancient
umbrellas and odd, ragged sticks.

The old man smiled at him, and he had eyes
as bright and sharp as a bird's. He seemed to
know what was wanted, for he at once took a
stick from his bundle. You would not have
said that it was the kind of stick that Bill was
looking for. It was short and heavy, and made
of some dark foreign wood; and instead of a
crook it had a handle shaped like a crescent, cut
out of a white substance which was neither bone
nor ivory. Yet Bill, as soon as he saw it, felt
that it was the one stick in the world for him.

" How much ? " he asked.

" One farthing," said the old man, and his
voice squeaked like a winter wind in a chimney.

Now a farthing is not a common coin, but
Bill happened to have one—a gift from Peter on
his arrival that day, along with a brass cannon,
five empty cartridges, a broken microscope, and
a badly-printed, brightly-illustrated narrative
called *Two Villains Foiled*. Peter was a famous
giver.

A farthing sounded too little, so Bill proffered
one of his scanty shillings.

" I said one farthing," said the old man rather snappishly.

The coin changed hands, and the little old man's wizened face seemed to light up with an elfin glee.

" 'Tis a fine stick, young sir," he squeaked; " a noble stick, when you gets used to the ways of it."

Bill had to run to catch up Thomas, who was plodding along with the dogs, now returned from their engagement.

" That's a queer chap—the old stick-man, I mean," he said.

" I ain't seen no old man, Maaster Bill," said Thomas. " What be 'ee talkin' about ? "

" The fellow back there. I bought this stick from him."

They both looked back, but there was no sign of any old man in the green lane. Indeed, if Bill had not been so absorbed in his purchase, he would have noticed that there was no sign of the hornbeam either. The lane ran bare between stone walls up to the hill pastures.

Thomas cast a puzzled glance at the stick. " That be a craafty stick, Maaster Bill——" But he said no more, for Bill had shaken it playfully at the dogs. As soon as they saw it they went off to keep another urgent engagement—

this time apparently with a long-distance hare —and Thomas was yelling and whistling for ten minutes before he brought them to heel.

It was a soft, grey afternoon, and Bill was stationed beside one of the deep dykes on the moor, well in cover of a thorn bush, while Thomas and the dogs departed on a circuit to show themselves beyond the big mere, so that the duck might move in Bill's direction. It was rather cold, and very wet under foot, for a lot of rain had fallen in the past week, and the mere, which was usually only a sedgy pond, had now grown to a great expanse of shallow flood-water.

Bill began his vigil in high excitement. He drove his new stick into the ground, and used the handle as a seat, while he rested his gun in the orthodox way in the crook of his arm. It was a double-barrelled 16-bore, and Bill knew that he would be lucky if he got a duck with it; but a duck was to him a bird of mystery, true wild game, and he preferred the chance of one to the certainty of many rabbits.

The minutes passed, the grey afternoon sky darkened towards twilight, but no duck came. Bill saw a wedge of geese high up in the air and longed to salute them. Also he heard snipe, but he could not locate them in the dim weather. There seemed to be redshank calling, too, which had no business there, for they should have been on the shore marshes. Far away he thought he detected the purring noise which Thomas made to stir the duck, but no overhead beat of wings followed.

It was so very quiet down there by the dyke that Bill began to feel eerie. The mood of eager anticipation died away, and he grew rather despondent. He would have been bored if he had not been slightly awed. He scrambled up the bank of the dyke and strained his eyes over the mere between the bare boughs of the thorn. He thought he saw duck moving. Yes, he was certain of it—they were coming from the direction of Thomas and the dogs. But they were not coming to him, and he realised what was happening. There was far too much water on the moor, and the birds, instead of flighting across the mere to the boundary slopes, were simply settling on the flood. From the misty waters came the rumour of many wildfowl.

CHAPTER TWO

THE ADVENTURE OF ALEMOOR

BILL came back to his wet stand grievously disappointed. He did not dare to leave it in case a flight did appear, but he had lost all hope. Gone now was the expectation of flourishing triumphantly a mallard, or a brace of mallard, before the sceptical eyes of his father and the admiring face of Peter. He tried to warm his feet by moving them up and down on the squelching turf, but his toes were icy and his boots were leaden. His gun was now under his arm, and he was fiddling idly with the handle of the stick, the point of which was embedded in the soil.

He made it revolve, and as it turned he said aloud—Bill had a trick of talking to himself—" I wish I was in the middle of the big flood."

Then a wonderful thing happened. Bill was not conscious of any movement, but suddenly his surroundings were completely changed. He had still his gun under his left arm and the stick in his right hand, but instead of standing on wet turf he was up to the waist in water. . . . And all around him were duck—shoveller, pintail, mallard, teal, widgeon, pochard, tufted—and bigger things that might be geese—swimming or diving or just alighting from the air.

Bill in his confusion understood one thing only, that his wish had been granted. He was in the very middle of the flood-water, and his one thought was how to take advantage of it.

He fired right and left at mallard, missing with his first barrel. Then the birds rose in alarm and he shoved in fresh cartridges and blazed wildly into the brown. His next two shots were at longer range, but he was certain that he had hit something. And then the duck vanished in the gloom, and he was left alone with the grey waters running out to the shadows.

He lifted up his voice and shouted wildly for Thomas and the dogs. He had got two anyhow—a mallard drake and a young teal, and he collected them. Then he saw something black about six yards off, and wading towards it he picked up a second mallard.

He stopped to listen, but the world had suddenly gone deathly quiet. Not a sound could be heard of Thomas whistling or the splashing of Gyp, the spaniel. He shouted again and again, but no answer came. The night seemed to make a thick curtain which blanketed his voice. Bill's moment of triumph began to change into acute fear.

Presently he discovered something which scared him worse. The flood waters were rising. The sluggish river Ale, which fed the mere, would be bringing down the rains from the hills. Bill knew what Alemoor could be when the floods were really out—a lake a mile or two in circumference, with twenty feet of water on what in summer were dry pastures. He realised very plainly that, unless he could get out before the floods deepened, he stood a very good chance of being drowned.

He had often been frightened in his life before, but he had never felt such panic as this. The trouble was that he did not know where the deeper mere lay—he had not a notion which was the quickest road to the dry land. But even in his fright he remembered his trophies. He had some string in his pocket, and he tied the three duck together so that he could hang them round his neck. Then he started plunging wildly in the direction from which he thought he had come.

The water was up to his armpits, and the draggled duck nearly choked him. Every now and then he would sink to his chin. Then suddenly he found himself soused over the head, and all but the last foot of his gun-barrel under water.

Bill, being a wet-bob at school, could swim, but swimming was impossible unless he dropped stick and gun, and even in his panic he would not relinquish his possessions. He trod water, and managed to struggle a yard or two till he found footing again and could get his breath. He was on some kind of mound or tussock of grass, and very warily he tried to feel his way forward. The ground rose beneath him and he found himself clear above the waist.

He halted for a moment to take a grip upon his fluttering nerves. In front of him lay floods, the colour of lead in the near distance and of ink beyond. The night had fallen and it would soon be black darkness.

Worse, the waters were still rising. Where he stood he felt them sucking every second a little higher up on his shivering body. . . . He lost hope and cried in a wild panic for Thomas. Then the tears came, unwilling tears, for Bill was not given to weeping. He felt horribly feeble, and would have fallen had he not leant on the stick, which was now deep beneath him in the quaking mire.

The stick ! The stick had brought him there
—could not the stick take him back ? What
had he done with it before ? . . . He had
twirled it and wished. He could not think
clearly, but surely that was what had happened.
. . . Bill's numb fingers with difficulty made
the point turn in the mud. " Oh, I wish I were
with Thomas," he sobbed. . . .

He *was* with Thomas. He found himself
sitting in about a foot of water, with Shawn, the
Irish setter, licking his face. Thomas himself
was as shapeless as a bush in the darkness, but
he had taken hold of Bill's arm and was helping
him to rise.

" Where in goodness ha' ye been, Maaster
Bill ? " the astounded keeper ejaculated.
" Them ducks was tigglin' out to the deep
water, and I was feared ye wouldn't get a shot.
Three on 'em, no less ! My word, ye 'ave
poonished 'em."

" I was in the deep water," said Bill, but he
could say no more, for all strength seemed
suddenly to go from him. He felt himself being
lifted in Thomas's arms and carried up the bank.
After that he was not very clear what happened.
Thomas had taken his gun from him and relieved him of the ducks, but nothing would
relax his clutch on the stick.

The evening's plan of entertainment was not carried out. There were no Hallowe'en festivities in the nursery, and Bill did not sit up for dinner. How he got home he never knew, but Thomas must have carried or dragged him up to the nearest farm, for he had a dim sense of being driven in a farmer's gig. He had no chance of exhibiting his bag to the family, even if he had had the strength, for he was promptly seized by an agitated mother and plunged into a hot bath with mustard in it. Then he was given something hot to drink. After that he knew nothing till he awoke late next morning, perfectly well, very hungry, but in every limb stiff as a poker.

He was not allowed to get up until just before luncheon, and, since Peter had been haled to church, he was left to his own thoughts. He was glad of that, for he wanted to be alone to think things out.

It was plain that a miracle had happened, a miracle connected with the stick. He had wished himself in the middle of the flood-water—he remembered that clearly—and at the time he had been doing something to the stick. What was it? It had been stuck in the ground and he had been playing with the handle. Yes, he had it! He had been turning it round when he uttered the wish.

Then the awful moments in the middle of the flood came back to him, but now he regarded them without horror. He had done the same thing there. He had turned the stick round and spoken his wish, and in a second had found himself with Thomas. . . . There was no doubt about it. Here was magic, and he was its master. Bill's mind was better stored with fairy-tales than with Latin and Greek, and he remembered many precedents.

He had a spasm of anxiety about the stick. The family were still at church, and he must make sure that it was safe, so he slipped on his dressing-gown and tiptoed downstairs to the hall, where he found it in the rack. He carried it up with him and hid it in the bottom of his playbox ; so precious a thing could not be left to the dangerous inquisition of Peter.

He was very quiet at luncheon, but he ate so heartily and looked so well that his mother's fears were dissipated. He was very quiet, too, at tea, and to his family's astonishment he volunteered to go to evening church, which would give him a chance for reflection. His conduct there was exemplary, for while Peter at his side had his usual Sunday attack of St.

Vitus's dance, Bill sat motionless as a mummy. On the way home his mother commented on it, and observed that Lower Chapel seemed to have taught him how to behave. But his thoughts during the service had not been devotional.

The stick lay beside him on the floor, and for a moment he had had a wild notion of twisting it during the Litany and disappearing for a few minutes to Kamschatka. Then prudence supervened. He must go very cautiously in this business, and court no questions. He would take the stick back to school and hide it in his room. He had a qualm when he thought what a " floater " it would be if a lower boy appeared with it in public. For him no more hours of boredom. School would no longer be a place of exile, but a rapturous holiday. He might slip home now and then and see what was happening—he would go often to Glenmore—he would visit any spot on the globe which took his fancy. His imagination reeled at the prospect, and he cloaked his chortles of delight in a fervent Amen.

CHAPTER THREE

THE ADVENTURE OF THE SOLOMON ISLANDS

NEXT morning, which was Monday, Bill awoke about an hour before dawn. This was not his usual custom, but he had gone to sleep so full of exciting thoughts that sleep did not altogether break their continuity. He lay for a while thinking. Before he could be quite sure of the powers of the new staff he must make another experiment, an experiment in cold blood, well-considered, premeditated. There was time for it before the family breakfast at nine.

He put on fives-shoes and a dressing-gown, got the stick out of the playbox, and tiptoed downstairs. He heard a housemaid moving in the direction of the dining-room and Groves opening the library shutters, but the hall was deserted. There was a garden door in the hall, of which the upper part was glass and now heavily shuttered. As quietly as he could, Bill undid the fastenings, wrestled with the key, and emerged into the foggy winter half-light.

It was bitterly cold, but it seemed to Bill essential that the experiment should be made out of doors, for there might be trouble if he appeared suddenly in the night-nursery on his return and confronted the eyes of Peter or Elsie. So he padded down the lawn to a retired half-moon of shrubbery beside the pond. His shoes were soon soaked with hoar-frost, and a passing dawn wind made him shiver and draw his dressing-gown around him. He had decided where to go, for in this kind of weather he yearned for heat. He plunged his stick in the turf.

" I want to be on the beach in the Solomon Islands," said Bill, and three times twisted the handle. . . .

His eyes seemed to dazzle with an excess of light, and something beat on his body like a blast from an open furnace. . . . Then he realised that he was standing on an expanse of blinding white sand, which a lazy blue sea was licking. Half a mile out were what looked like reefs, with a creamy crest of spindrift. Behind him, at a distance of perhaps two hundred yards, was a belt of high green forest out of which stuck a tall feather of palms. A hot wind was blowing and tossing the tree-tops, but it only crisped the farther sea and did not break the mirror of the lagoon.

Bill gasped for joy to find his dream fulfilled. He was in the Far Pacific, where he had always longed to be. In the forest behind him there must be all kinds of wonderful fruits and queer beasts and birds. He calculated that he had nearly an hour to spend, and might at any rate penetrate the fringes of its green mysteries.

But in the meantime he was very hot and could not endure the weight of winter pyjamas and a winter dressing-gown. Also he longed to bathe in those inviting waters. So he shed everything and hopped gaily down to the tide's edge, leaving the stick still upright in the sand.

The sea felt as delicious as it looked, but Bill, though a good swimmer, kept near the edge for fear of sharks. This was very different from the chill flood-waters of Alemoor. He looked down through blue depths to a floor like marble, and the water was a caress. Bill wallowed and splashed, with the fresh salt smell, which he loved, in his nostrils.

By and by he ventured a little farther out, and floated on his back, looking up at the pale, hot sky. For a little he was unconscious of the passage of time, as he drifted on the aromatic tide. Then he saw a little reef close at hand, and was just on the point of striking out for it when he cast a glance back towards the shore.

Bill got the fright of his life, for at the edge of the forest stood men—dark-skinned men—armed with spears. He had forgotten that these islands might have other things in them besides strange fruits and birds and beasts.

They had halted and were looking at his stick, but apparently they had not yet seen him. Supposing they got the stick, what on earth would happen ? With a fluttering heart Bill made for the shore.

As soon as he was in shallow water the men caught sight of him and moved forward. He was perhaps fifty yards from the stick, which cast its long morning shadow on the sand, and they were two hundred yards on the farther side. At all costs he must get to it first. He sprang out of the sea, and as he ran he saw to his horror that the men ran also—ran in great bounds, shouting and brandishing their spears.

His little naked body scurried up the sand. The fifty yards seemed miles, and it was an awful thing to run towards those savage faces and not away from them. Bill felt his legs giving way beneath him, as in his nightmares, when he had found himself on a railway track with an express approaching and could scarcely move. But he ran faster than he thought, and before he knew had laid a quivering hand on the stick.

No time to put on his clothes. He managed to grab his dressing-gown with one hand and the stick with the other, and as he twirled the handle a spear whizzed by his ear.

" I want to be home," he gasped, and the next second he stood naked between the shrubbery and the pond, clutching his dressing-gown. The Solomon Islanders had got his pyjamas and his fives-shoes, and I wonder what they made of them !

The cold of a November morning brought him quickly to his senses. He clothed his shivering body in his dressing-gown and ran by devious paths to the house. But this time the hall was clearly not for him. Happily the gun-room door was unlocked, and he was able to ascend by way of empty passages and back-stairs to the nursery floor.

He did not, however, escape the eagle eye of Elsie, the nurse, who read a commination

HE SPRANG OUT OF THE SEA, AND AS HE RAN HE SAW TO HIS HORROR THAT THE MEN RAN ALSO——RAN IN GREAT BOUNDS, SHOUTING AND BRANDISHING THEIR SPEARS.

service over a boy who went out of doors imperfectly clad on such a morning. She pro-
phesied pneumonia and plumped him into
a hot bath.

Bill applied his tongue to the back of his hand.
Yes, it tasted salt, and the salt smell was still
in his nose. It had not been a dream. . . .
He hugged himself in the bath and made strange
gurgling sounds of joy. The experiment had
been brilliantly successful, and the magic of the
staff was amply proved. But he must go carefully, very carefully. He had suddenly an
awful reminiscence of fearsome black faces and
bloodshot eyes.

Events that morning did not go according to
programme. There was no walk with the dogs,
for Bill was in disgrace. Elsie wailed for lost
pyjamas, of which he could give no account.
Under cross-examination he was, as the newspapers say, reticent. He avoided Peter and
spent the time before departure in wrapping up
his new stick in many layers of brown paper
and tying it firmly with string. In this way
he thought he might safely carry it back to
school.

But in the bustle of leaving it was somehow
left behind, and Bill only discovered his loss

when he was half-way to London. The discovery put him into a fever of anxiety. He could not go back for it, and there was the awful risk that in his absence Peter or Groves or some other interfering person might monkey with it. Or it might get lost. Deep gloom settled upon his spirit. At luncheon he was so morose that Aunt Alice, who had strong and unorthodox views about education, observed that he seemed to be a clear proof that the public school system was a failure.

Without the stick there were none of the delights for Bill over which he had gloated in church. His first idea was to have it sent to him, but that seemed too risky. In the past various parcels, despatched by rail or post, had gone astray. Nor was there the chance of a visit from someone at home, for his mother and father and Peter presently went up to London for several weeks.

So Bill wrote to Groves, the butler, a very ill-spelt letter, demanding that he should find the brown paper parcel and put it securely in his playbox. He enclosed one of his scanty stamps for a reply. It was four days before the answer came, and it did something to relieve Bill's anxiety. The parcel had been found—awful thought ! in Peter's playbox—and Groves had duly stowed it away as directed.   Bill breathed freely again.

But the last weeks of that half lacked gaiety. His disappointment died away, but he had many spasms of anxiety.   He counted the days to the Christmas holidays.

CHAPTER FOUR

THE ADVENTURE OF GLENMORE

ON the 19th day of December Bill returned from school in time for luncheon. Never before had he looked forward so wildly to getting home again. He greeted his mother with the most perfunctory caress, dodged Peter, and rushed upstairs to his playbox. Thank Heaven, the stick was safely there ! He tore off the brown paper wrappings and carried it down to the gun-room, where he put it in a special place beside his 16-bore.

It being the first day of holiday, according to fashion the afternoon was spent in a family walk. It was decided that Bill and Peter should set off together and should join the others at a place called the Roman Camp. " Let the boys have a chance of being alone," his father said.

This exactly suited Bill's book, and as they left the dining-room he clutched his small brother. " Shrimp," he said in his ear, " you are going to have the afternoon of your life."

It was a bright, mild day, with the leafless woods and the brown plough-lands lit by a pale December sun. Peter, as he trotted beside him, jerked out breathless enquiries about what Bill proposed to do, and was told to wait and see. Their sister's dog had joined them. This was a cairn terrier called Catsbane, because of his extraordinary dislike for cats, and he did not often honour the boys with his company. He was much beloved by Barbara, and Peter felt a certain responsibility for his conduct, and was always yelling and whistling him to heel.

Arrived at a clump of beeches which promised privacy, Bill first swore his brother to secrecy with the most awful oaths that he could imagine.

" Put your arm round my waist and hang on to my belt," he told him. " I'm going to take you to have a look at Glenmore."

" Don't be silly," said Peter. " That only happens in summer, and besides we haven't packed yet."

" Shut up and hold tight," said Bill.

But at the last moment anxiety for Catsbane overcame Peter ; and so it befell that as Bill twirled the stick and spoke the necessary words, Peter was clutching Catsbane's collar. . . .

The boys were looking not at the smooth boles of beeches, but at a little coppice of rowans and birches above the narrow glen of a hill burn. It was Glenmore in very truth. There was the strip of mossy lawn and the whitewashed gable-end of the lodge ; there to the left, beside the walled garden, was the smoking chimney of the head stalker's cottage ; there beyond the trees was the long lift of brown moorland and the peak of Stob Ghabhar. Stob Ghabhar had snow on its summit, which the boys had never seen before. To them Glenmore was the true home of the soul, but they knew it only in the glory of late summer and early autumn. In its winter dress it seemed for a moment strange. Then the sight of an old collie waddling across the lawn gave the connecting link.

" There's Wattie," Peter gasped, and lifted up his voice in an excited summons.

His brother promptly scragged him. " Don't be an ass, Shrimp," he said fiercely. " This is a secret, you fathead. This is magic. Nobody must know we are here. Come on and explore."

But Wattie had seen Catsbane, and the two dogs held high converse together. In the autumn they had always been friends. Catsbane was a proud animal and would have nothing to do with the retrievers or the stable terrier, but for some reason or another he was partial to Wattie. The two went off down the burnside.

"Here, this'll never do," said Peter. "Catsbane may not come back till to-morrow morning —he's done it before."

But there was no help for it, for the dogs had already disappeared in the thicket, and the boys were too full of excitement to have much care for the future. For an hour—it must have been an hour, Bill calculated afterwards, but it seemed like ten minutes—they visited their favourite haunts. They found the robber's cave in the glen where a raven nested, and the pool where Bill had got his first big trout, and the stretch of the river from which their father that year had had the 30-pound salmon. Then they dipped into the big fir wood which clothed the hillside. There were no blaeberries or crowberries now, but there were many woodcock. After that Bill had a shot with his catapult at a wicked old blackcock on a peat-stack. Then they found Wattie the collie, who had shaken himself loose from Catsbane, and induced him to make a third in the party.

Peter moaned about Catsbane. "What'll we

say to Barbara? He's lost now—we'll never get him back."

But Bill only said, "Confound the beastly pup," and had a shot at a stray pheasant.

All their motions were as stealthy as an Indian's, and the climax of the adventure was reached when they shed Wattie, climbed the garden wall, and looked in at the window of the keeper's cottage.

Tea was laid before a bright peat fire in the parlour, so Mrs. Macrae must be expecting company. It looked a very good tea, for there were scones and pancakes and shortbread and currant loaf and heather honey. Both boys suddenly felt famished at the sight.

"Mrs. Macrae always gives me a scone and honey," Peter bleated. "I'm hungry. I want one."

So did Bill. His soul longed for food, but he kept hold of his prudence. "We dare not show ourselves," he whispered. "But perhaps we might pinch a scone. It would not be stealing, for if Mrs. Macrae saw us she'd say, ' Come awa in, laddies, and get a jeely piece.' I'll give you a back, Shrimp, and in you get."

The window was opened, and Peter was hoisted through, falling with a bang on a patch-work rug. But he never reached the table, for at that moment the parlour door opened and someone entered.

After that things happened fast. Peter, urged by Bill's anguished whisper, turned back to the window and was hauled through by the scruff of the neck. A woman's voice was heard crying—" Mercy on us, it's the bairns ! " as the culprits darted into the shelter of the gooseberry bushes.

Bill realised that there was no safety in the garden, so he dragged Peter over the wall by the way they had come, thereby seriously damaging a pear tree. But they had been observed, and, as they scrambled out of a rose bed, they heard cries, and saw Mrs. Macrae appearing round the end of the wall, having come through the stable-yard. Also a figure, which looked like Angus the river gillie, was running from the same direction.

There was nothing for it but to go. Bill seized Peter with one hand and the stick with the other and spoke the words, with Angus not six yards away. . . . As he looked once more at the familiar beech boles, his ears were still filled with the cries of an excited woman and the frenzied barking of Wattie the collie.

The two boys, very warm and flustered, and

rather scratched about the hands and legs, confronted their father and mother and their sister Barbara, who was eighteen and very proud.

" Hullo, hullo ! " they heard their father say. " I thought you were hiding somewhere hereabouts. You young rascals know how to take cover, for you seemed to spring out of the ground. You look as if you had been playing football. Better walk home with us and cool down. . . . Bless my soul, Peter, what's that you have got ? It's bog myrtle ! Where on earth did you find it ? I have never seen it before in Oxfordshire ! "

Then Barbara raised a ladylike voice. " Oh, Mummie, look at the mess they've made of themselves ! They've been among the brambles. Peter has two holes in his stocking. Just look at Bill's hands ! " And she wrinkled her finical nose and sniffed.

Bill kept a diplomatic silence, and Peter, usually garrulous, did the same, for his small wrist was in his brother's savage clutch.

Then Barbara bethought herself of Catsbane. " Where's my dog ? " she cried. " You know he started out with you. You wretched boys have lost him ! "

There was a great hunt for Catsbane, but of course he could not be found. " I know where he is," said Barbara bitterly. " He's gone down to Johnson's farm and has probably by this time killed twenty chickens. Or he's at the badger's earth in Yewbarrow wood."

Bill's desperate grip only just prevented Peter from laughing.

CHAPTER FIVE

THE ADVENTURE OF CATSBANE

TEA was a difficult meal. Peter was in a state of high excitement, gurgling to himself and casting secret conspiratorial glances at Bill, which Barbara intercepted. Barbara was in distress about her dog, and she read in Peter's behaviour some guilty knowledge of its whereabouts. She cross-examined him severely, but Peter only giggled, and Barbara became very cross indeed.

Bill realised that something must be done about Catsbane, and done at once. If he were left loose in the Highlands he would be found, and people would naturally enquire what had suddenly shifted a cairn terrier five hundred miles farther north. So he fled from Peter and sought the darkness of the garden, twirled the stick, and wished himself at Glenmore. . . .

He ought to have wished himself where Catsbane was, but the idea never occurred to him. Where he asked to be was the vicinity of the house of Hector, the second stalker, which was behind the kennels. He had seen the terrier moving in that direction, and it used to be a favourite haunt of his.

He found himself in the midst of a soft flurry of snow. When he had left Glenmore several hours earlier it had been fine weather, but the clouds had been banking up in the north. Now the snow had come, and since it was falling steadily it would be a business to find an inconspicuous white dog. The lights were lit in Hector's cottage, and the door was open. Bill snuggled up in the darkness against the wall and observed two men standing at the threshold. One was Hector himself, and the other looked like Angus, the river gillie. The lamplight from within fell on Hector's face, and it was very grave.

"She's bad," Hector was saying. "She's awfu' bad. We maun get the doctor or she'll be bye wi' it. The puir thing's greetin' wi' pain. Haste ye, Angus, and awa' on your bicycle to Abercailly and bring Dr. Porteous back wi' ye. If he's no at hame ye maun range the countryside till ye find him. Oh, man, hurry! I daurna' leave her, or I'd be off mysel'."

"But ma bicycle's broke," said Angus glumly. "I ran into a stane last nicht, and the front wheel's like a peaseweep's egg."

" Then awa' up the glen to Jock Rorison, the herd, and borrow his. There's nae other bicycle about the place. Oh, man, haste ye, or ye'll be ower late."

Bill saw Angus start off at a trot and Hector turn wearily indoors. He was alarmed by the news, for he had been fond of Mrs. Hector, who had often stayed him and Peter with oatcakes and jam. . . . And then suddenly a great idea occurred to him. Abercailly was five miles off, and Angus and his bicycle would take nearly an hour to reach it in the snow. But he had the staff and could be there in a second. . . . He twirled it and wished himself in Dr. Porteous's back garden.

The doctor knew him by sight, and it would never do to reveal himself. He must approach the back door and pretend to be one of the cottagers' boys from Glenmore. The darkness and the snow were in his favour. So Bill turned up the collar of his jacket and knocked loudly.

It seemed a long time before Dr. Porteous's housekeeper opened. She peered into the night. " Wha is it ? " she asked, blinking her eyes.

Now Bill, who had a good ear, had always

prided himself on his command of the Scots tongue. This was the moment for its use.

" It's me," he said, in the lilting tone of the countryside. " I'm frae Glenmore. Hector Cameron's wife's lyin' awfu' bad, and they sent me to tell the doctor that he maun come at once or she'll dee."

" Mercy ! that's bad news," said the housekeeper. " The doctor's indoors haein' his tea. He's had an awfu' hard day, and he'll be sweir to gang out in the snaw. But needs must if Ailie Cameron's bad. D'ye ken what the trouble is ? "

" I never heard," said Bill, " but she's greetin' sair wi' pain, and Hector Cameron's in an awfu' way about it. He said I was to get the doctor at a' costs, though I had to look for him ower the hale parish."

" Is it as bad as that ? I'll awa and tell him. Ye can come in and wait by the kitchen fire."

" I think I'll bide here. Ye see, I'm terrible wat."

A minute later the housekeeper returned. " The doctor will stert in the car as sune as he's got his buits on. Wad ye like a piece ? "

" Thank ye, mem," said Bill, " but I had my tea afore I left." And without more words he turned into the darkness.

So far, so good, Bill reflected. Dr. Porteous would be at Glenmore before Angus had well started on the herd's bicycle. Bill felt a glow of conscious merit, the surprised glow of one who has slipped accidentally into virtue.

Now for Catsbane. Bill's wits had returned to him, and as he turned the stick he wished to be beside the dog. . . .

He found himself in an extraordinary place. He seemed to be high up on a hillside, but the snow was falling so fast that he could not discover his whereabouts. The ground was a tangle of boulders deep in blaeberries and long heather and of old stumps of trees. He could only think that it was the fir wood on the slopes of Stob Ghabhar, which had been cut down in the summer.

There beside him was Catsbane. The little dog was furiously busy, trying to force his way into a hole below a big stone. Bill could not see him properly because of the darkness and the snow. But he could hear him panting, and, feeling for him, he discovered the stump of his tail. Bill caught the tail and pulled out an excessively dirty and protesting terrier.

" You dirty little beast," he said. " You're for it, you know. You'll have to be washed, and you hate that."

Catsbane barked furiously.

" I don't blame you," said Bill, relenting. " You're after a fox, and you can't hunt foxes at home."

So he seized Catsbane by the scruff and twirled the stick, and the two found themselves back beside the pond in the garden.

It was a still, dry night and mild, very different from the tempest of Glenmore. Catsbane shook himself vigorously, and as they came into the light below the library window Bill saw that he was black with soil and as wet as a bath sponge.

" I've found your dog," he told Barbara as he entered the hall.

The much-relieved owner seized upon the grimy fragment of terrier and clasped it to her breast; but she dropped it hastily. " Catsbane, where on earth have you been ? " she cried. " You've been on Alemoor and you've been down a rabbit-hole, and I believe you've been fighting, for your ear's cut. Oh, Daddy ! " she added, as her father appeared, " did you ever see such a disreputable little dog ? "

Catsbane had shaken himself again and was now standing shivering in the glow of the hall fire. Bill's father took him up and looked at him curiously.

" This is the second miracle that has happened to-day," he said. " First you boys find bog myrtle, and now Catsbane has discovered peat. He's been rolling in it, and there isn't any peat within fifty miles ! "

CHAPTER SIX

"BEAUTY" AND "BANDS"

THREE days later at breakfast Bill's father looked up from his letters.

"Glenmore seems to have become demented," he said. "First I had a wire from Mrs. Macrae." He fumbled in his pocket and produced a pink slip.

"'*Is the bairns alright. Macrae.*' The honest woman does not waste words. I could make nothing of it, and thought it might be a new kind of Christmas greeting. But here's the explanation in her letter. It seems that Glenmore is haunted, and by such fearsome spectres as Bill and Peter. They were seen three nights ago in Mrs. Macrae's best room by Mrs. Macrae herself, and afterwards in the garden by Angus as well. She says that Angus was not a yard off when they disappeared, and that he saw their faces quite clear and could describe what they were wearing. It seems that the whole glen is solemnised. I wired at once that the boys were perfectly well, but Mrs. Macrae is not satisfied. She thinks it may be a fore-warning of coming disaster, and she implores me never to take my eyes off them till Hogmanay is past."

Bill's mother looked anxious. " What an extraordinary thing ! I always thought Mrs. Macrae a pillar of common sense. She hasn't second sight, has she ? "

" If she has, I don't suppose Angus has it, and they both saw the ghosts. They were solid enough ghosts, for they knocked a stone off the wall and broke the branch of a pear tree. A couple of Abercailly boys on the loose ! Bill, did you know that you had a double in Abercailly ? "

Bill grinned sheepishly and said nothing. He had begun to realise that in this business of the magic staff he must walk delicately and pro-voke no questions. Any future enterprise must be carefully thought out in all its bearings. He had already passed a self-denying ordinance, and had made no experiment since the rescue of Catsbane.

" Does she say anything about Mrs. Cameron ? " he heard his mother ask.

" Yes. She is not out of danger, but the reports are good. Apparently they got her to Abercailly and operated in the nick of time.

That was the evening they saw the ghosts, and naturally Mrs. Macrae's mind was keyed up for marvels. You had better write to her, Jean, and say the boys are all right. She will believe you sooner than me."

Then Barbara, to Bill's disquiet, put in an unwanted oar. "That was the evening that Catsbane was lost and came back covered with peat. You remember, Daddy? And the boys found bog myrtle!"

After tea Bill was allowed for a treat to sit in the library and study the pictures in the big bird book. His father sat in an armchair with an old calf-bound folio on his knee, from which he appeared to be taking notes. From time to time he made ejaculations of interest or surprise, and once he said, " Bless my soul, what a queer story! "

Several times he got up to refer to other books among the thousands which lined the great room. Then at last he startled Bill out of his contemplation of a coloured plate of the red-necked phalarope by dropping the folio on the floor. He stood up on the hearth-rug, filled his pipe from a box on the mantelpiece, and looked down at Bill.

" I have just come across a very good

story," he said. "Would you like to hear it?"

He took down from a shelf a slim black volume and found a passage. "Read that," he said.

Bill read:

"*Et assumpsi mihi duas virgas, unam vocavi Decorem, et alteram vocavi Funiculum; et pavi gregem.*"

"Now have a shot at construing it."

Bill had a shot, but he did not succeed. Latin was not his strong suit, and half the words were unfamiliar.

His father handed him a Bible. "Look up the seventh verse of the eleventh chapter of Zechariah and read."

Bill read:

"And I took unto me two staves, the one I called Beauty, and the other I called Bands; and I fed the flock."

"You understand that?" his father said. "The prophet had two staves, one called *Decor* and the other *Funiculus;* that is 'Beauty' and 'Bands.' One was for comfort and the other for discipline—you might say one was a walking-stick and the other a schoolmaster's cane. Now the book I have been reading—it is a volume of *Acta Sanctorum*, the 'Doings of the Saints,' and it was written in Germany in the twelfth century

—says that these staves were real sticks and that they had magical power. They lay in the treasury in the Temple of Jerusalem until the Emperor Titus sacked it and carried them off. After that they seem to have roamed for centuries about Europe. Charlemagne—you have heard of Charlemagne ?—had one, and the Emperor Justinian had one ; but they were never lóng in one place. Sometimes a Pope got hold of them, and sometimes a Bishop, and sometimes a King, and sometimes a peasant, but they disappeared as soon as they were misused. The point about them was that they were magic sticks and would carry their possessor anywhere in the world he wanted to go to. But the trouble was that you could not be certain what was their particular magic. They were as alike as two peas, but one was *Decor* and the other *Funiculus*, and if you treated *Decor* like *Funiculus* it took the huff and disappeared. If it was *Decor* it would take you gallivanting about the earth for your amusement and never complain. But if you used it for some big serious job, it was apt to leave you in the lurch. *Funiculus* was just the opposite. It was all right in things like battles and rescues and escapes, but if you took it on a pleasure trip it would let you down."

Bill listened with breathless interest. " What happened to the sticks ? " he asked.

" My book says that in its time, that is the twelfth century, *Funiculus* had gone over the horizon, but *Decor* was believed to be in the possession of the Emperor Frederick. . . . It's a good story, isn't it ? I dare say it is the origin of all the old witches' broomsticks in the fairy tales. But these were broomsticks with wills of their own. . . . Hullo ! hullo ! it's six o'clock. I must see Thomas about to-morrow's covert shoot."

When his father had left, Bill sat for a long time in meditation. Clearly he had got one of the two staves which had come down from the old prophet in the Bible and had drifted for two thousand years through the hands of Popes and Kings. The question was, which one ? Was it *Beauty* or *Bands* ?

Bill was a conscientious thinker, and set himself to analyse his experiences. The adventures of Alemoor and the Solomon Islands had been more or less undertaken for his own amusement, and so had the first visit to Glenmore. On the other hand, the rescue of Catsbane and the summoning of the doctor to Mrs. Cameron had had a distinct flavour of duty. As yet there was not enough evidence to decide which staff he had got. It would have been an awful business if he had used it wrongly and it had objected; Bill shuddered when he remembered the faces of the South Sea Islanders. Perhaps he was being allowed a trial trip to test him. On the whole, he decided that this was the likeliest explanation. But the time of probation was probably now over, since he knew about the staff's peculiarities. He had an eerie feeling that some fate had led his father to discover that story in the funny old book.

Bill found the page in it which his father had marked, but he could make nothing of the close black type and the queer Latin. Then he read again the passage in Zechariah. For a long time he thought hard, till Groves came in to make up the fire and to warn him that his supper was ready. He had reached the conclusion that the next experiment must combine somehow the partialities of both Beauty and Bands, for he could not afford to make a mistake.

Next morning he overheard a conversation between his father and his mother. His father seemed to be very angry.

"It is getting simply intolerable. Those disgusting Benisons have been at their monkey tricks again. It appears that there was a biggish party at Yardley last week-end, to meet the Viceroy, who was at school with the General. What did the bright young Benisons do but make a raid in the middle of the Saturday night ! They managed to burgle the back premises, and flung every scrap of food in the house into the moat, leaving an idiotic doggerel poem in the butler's pantry. Yardley is ten miles from a town, so you may imagine the trouble about the commissariat on the Sunday. The General went raving mad, and started out for Wildash with a horsewhip ; but he thought better of it and turned back. What could he do ? They would only laugh at the old fellow. He talks about prosecuting ; but it won't be easy to bring the charge home, for the brutes are pretty clever. I wish to heaven somebody would retaliate in kind and give those jokers a taste of their own medicine."

Bill pricked up his ears. He knew all about the Benisons, who five years before had bought Wildash from a long-descended bankrupt squire. They were his father's nearest neighbours, but there was no commerce between the two houses. The elder Benison had made a great deal of money in the City during the War, and had brought his flock of glossy sons and over-decorated daughters to an old-fashioned place which was not glossy or decorated. They were only at Wildash for a few weeks in the winter, but they contrived to crowd these weeks with scandals. They had enormous raffish house parties, and their chief amusement consisted in playing practical jokes on inoffensive neighbours. The countryside detested them, for they spent nothing in the village, which was badly neglected, and gave not a penny to local purposes.

At first the sons and daughters had gone out hunting on expensive horses, but their manners were so vile that the Master, in a moment of expansion, had told them that they were only fit to hunt jackals on jackasses round the walls of Jerusalem.

But they kept the neighbourhood from boredom, for they were the theme of endless gossip. Bill had heard all about "them Ben'sons" and their doings from his village friends, who were at once horrified and exhilarated by beings unlike any gentry they had ever known. That very morning old Noggin, the blacksmith, had been recounting the wonders of a dance to be held at Wildash on Christmas Eve.

"They do say, Maaster Bill," Noggin had declared, "as how the young gen'men is going to dress themsels up as devils with tails.   There can't be no blessing on them belltinkerings."

Noggin was a Primitive Methodist, much given to the use of Scripture phrases, but he did not know that the word " belltinkering " came straight down from the Baal-worship of the hoariest antiquity.

Bill fell into a happy muse.   Here might be the chance of an adventure which *Beauty* would welcome, and of which *Bands* would not disapprove.

CHAPTER SEVEN

THE ADVENTURE OF THE
CHRISTMAS PARTY—I

THAT afternoon Bill went for a walk through the fields to Wildash, which lay two miles off in the valley. The Hall, a massive early Georgian building, had a park on three sides of it, but on the fourth it snuggled up to the village ; indeed, its stables and out-houses abutted on the village street. In that street lived, with his mother, a friend of Bill's, 'Erb by name, with whom he had often gone fishing and bird-nesting. 'Erb was pantry boy at the big house, but only when the Benisons were in residence, for at other times he was learning to be a carpenter. He slept at the Hall, but Bill knew that it was his custom to resort to his mother's cottage for tea.

Bill had tea with 'Erb and sounded him about the Benisons' Christmas festivities, on which his friend expanded with round eyes. The family were expected at the Hall next day, which was December 24th, and they were bringing with them enough guests to fill every bedroom. Mr. Blett, the butler, was in London that day with Roberts, the first footman, supervising the preparations. On Christmas Eve the party was not to dine until ten o'clock, and the revels were to be kept up all night, supper being at the hour at which ordinary people breakfasted. 'Erb was full of marvellous details about the costumes to be worn, and the escapades which might be expected. The dining-room was to be transformed into the similitude of a dungeon, with blue lights burning, and—said 'Erb in awed tones—they were going to drink the wine out of skulls.

Bill asked about the servants' meal. That wasn't to be forgotten, said 'Erb. The upper servants were to dine in the housekeeper's room, and the lower in the servants' hall, three-quarters of an hour before the main dinner. The Benisons, it appeared, did not, on such occasions, rely much on their own cookery, and the chief dishes were coming down from London.

" Most of 'em cold," said 'Erb. " They don't fancy a nice bit of 'ot meat, like me. It ain't food they cares for so much as the pop."

" What's that ? " Bill asked.

" Wine," said 'Erb, darkly. " That's what

Mr. Blett's looking after. He's bringing down loads of it. That's what they drinks mostly. ' A bottle of pop,' says Mr. Lionel when he feels nohow. Mr. Reggie he sticks to brandy."

Bill accompanied 'Erb in his walk up to the Hall in the frosty twilight, and, since the family was not at home and Mr. Blett was absent, he was allowed indoors. 'Erb was a little nervous about his visitor, until he discovered that the kitchen staff were entertaining guests on their own account, and that the second footman had gone off on his bicycle to see his sweetheart.

The two boys roamed about the cavernous servants' quarters, which had been built in the days when each squire of Wildash sat in Parliament for the county, and generously entertained his constituents. He was shown 'Erb's cubbyhole behind the main butler's pantry, and was permitted to glance inside the great wine-cellars. They seemed ill-stocked, and 'Erb explained the reason. " The family don't care for wine— port and them kinds—what Mr. Blett says is ' wine indeed '—only for that there pop. And Mr. Blett says they don't keep much of it 'ere, for the cellars ain't dry enough. That's why he's gone to London." But some of the pop was already there, stacked on the pantry floor in wooden boxes with odd marks on them.

Bill made a careful inspection on his own account of the back premises of the Hall. He noticed that all the windows were heavily barred, so that it would be impossible to climb in or out. He observed, too, with satisfaction, that there were keys on all the inner doors and that these keys were on the outside.

He begged to be allowed a glimpse of the rest of the house, and 'Erb rather uneasily complied. The passage which led to it did not terminate in an ordinary green-baize door as in Bill's own home, but in a solid wooden affair which was equipped with lock and key. Beyond this was a small alcove with a hatch opening into the dining-room. Clearly, if this door were once barred, all communication would be cut off between the back premises and the main apartments.

There was not much to be seen, for the huge pillared hall was littered with furniture, which, for some reason, had been turned out of the library. But a peep into the dining-room was sensational. 'Erb snapped a switch and Bill saw that all the lights were fantastically coloured, and that the big chandelier in the centre burned with an unearthly crimson glow. The pictures had been taken down and the walls covered with a cloth to resemble rough stone, and there was a contraption at one end which looked like a stage.

'Erb was slightly awed. " Crikcy ! " he said. " This ain't the place I'd pick to cat my meat in. But there's no accounting for the gentry's taste."

After that Bill was hustled back to humble life. 'Erb was nervous in case the kitchen tea-party should break up or the second footman return from his love-making. " Nip along, Master Bill," he urged. " There's funny folks in this 'ouse, and Mr. Blett would have my ears off if he 'eard I'd let anyone in."

So Bill took his leave, and only just in time, for by a rapid retreat into a laurel bush he narrowly escaped the returning footman.

On his way home he paid a visit to another friend, Pobjoy, the earth-stopper, who was a brother-in-law of Thomas, his father's keeper. He knew that at this hour Pobjoy would be busy in the lee of Wildash Great Spinney, and sure enough he found a figure like an ancient gnome, bending over his traps at the end of Lemming's Lane. The figure was attended by a ferocious mongrel called Jum. But Jum was an ally of Bill's and treated him kindly.

He waited until Pobjoy had finished his task, and then accompanied him to his cottage on the other side of the wood. A great plan had suddenly dawned upon Bill's mind, and he wanted information. Pobjoy gave it him.

The Wildash Pig Club was to have its supper in the schoolroom on Christmas Eve. It was not a flourishing pig club ; indeed, its finances were chronically unhealthy, but it clung to its antique custom of an annual feast. Bill knew all the members : his own Thomas was one, and Noggin the blacksmith, and Lippett the road-man, and Amos Tuck the postman, and Martin the ditcher, and the shepherd from Coldeaston, and the under-keeper from Wardsley, and Springwell the thatcher. Of this fraternity of gnarled worthies Pobjoy was President. None of the Hall servants belonged to the Club. Mr. Benison had only bought the house and a few paddocks, and his grooms and chauffeurs did not mix in local society.

Pobjoy was eloquent on the Club's poverty. " I've seen the day, Maaster Bill, when twenty lads'd sit down to a smoking loin of pork, and a roast of beef, and a great stew of wild-jucks, and a pigeon pie as big as a horse trough, and old Squire John'd send down lashins of right strong ale from his own buttery. Now, by gob !

we're hard put to it to get some cold pig food and some of them skimpy little meat pies as Hutt the baker makes. They be hard times for us poor folks."

" Doesn't Mr. Benison help ? " Bill asked.

" Help ! " Pobjoy spat savagely. " Them Ben'sons ! They keep their own pig club up at the Hall, and I wish their guzzling may choke 'em. They take no more concern in the parish than a gor-crow that happens over from Alemoor to pick up a pullet. . . . And the beer nowadays ! "

Pobjoy became savagely reminiscent. " That hog-wash from the ' Plough and 'Arrow ' ain't beer, for it don't comfort the innards. A man might drink three buckets of it and be none the merrier."

Bill enquired about the hour of the supper, and was told ten o'clock.

" The Wardsley lads can't come before. . . . See here, Maaster Bill, you pass that word on to your Thomas. We used to sit down at nine. I don't want Thomas to get his shins cold waiting."

With a new confidence Bill watched Pobjoy swing his traps from his shoulder and stamp his feet at his doorstep. He hotly disliked intruders like the Benisons, and he had a furious affection for his own people. *Beauty* could not be averse to the joyous enterprise which he meditated, and *Bands* must approve its stern moral purpose. There was a lot in the Bible about humbling the proud and exalting the humble.

CHAPTER EIGHT

THE ADVENTURE OF THE
CHRISTMAS PARTY—II

CHRISTMAS EVE was very cold. Up till then there had been a mild frost with a wind in the north, but on that afternoon the wind swung round to the east and the clouds massed for snow. On Christmas Eve it was the custom for Bill to go to bed at the same time as Peter, and with the expectation of Santa Claus he usually went without protest. Bill was by this time a sceptic on the subject of the visit of the Saint, though Peter was still a devout believer. He knew that his mother would come to his bedside about eleven to fill his stocking, for he had once been awake and caught her in the act.

All this was as it should be. The period between 9 and 10.30 was going to be for him a time of stern endeavour. He had occasional spasms of nervousness, which he quieted by reminding himself that whatever happened he was perfectly safe, if he only kept his head.

Whether his staff were *Beauty* or *Bands* it could not fail him, since the enterprise combined all the purposes of both.

Bill put on stout knickerbockers and a sweater, for the weather was sharp, and at the same time he dared not cumber himself with too many garments. On his feet were fives-shoes. Then he twirled the stick and wished himself just outside the Hall dining-room windows, and in a second he was standing on gravel which was beginning to be powdered with snow.

The windows were not shuttered, and within a big fire was blazing, which gave light enough to reveal a table loaded with dishes, and another assortment on a long sideboard. A second sideboard held a forest of bottles and glasses, and below it were further bottles in great wine-coolers. There were several gramophones going in the bedrooms, and a great deal of laughter in one of the upper rooms. The inmates would be preparing for dinner, Bill decided, and getting into the fantastic costumes with which rumour had been busy.

Bill padded along the house-back till he reached the servants' quarters. He made out the butler's pantry, which he had marked down the evening before by the clump of winter-jasmine outside it. That gave him his bearings and enabled him to locate the housekeeper's room. In this part of the house the windows were all shuttered and barred, and when he tried the main door he found it locked. There were sounds of many voices inside—no doubt, the staff assembling for their meal. This, he knew, was to be in two places, the servants' hall and the housekeeper's room. He stood and pondered for a moment till he remembered the exact lie of these apartments.

Then he made the magic stick take him inside 'Erb's cubby-hole, as the safest base of operations. A second earlier and he would have landed on the top of 'Erb, who was just closing the door behind him.

Bill waited till the footsteps died away in the flagged passage, and then stealthily proceeded to reconnoitre. The humbler diners had assembled. He listened outside the housekeeper's room, and heard Mrs. Chalk, the housekeeper, who was a Seventh Day Baptist, saying grace. He listened outside the servants' hall, and heard a cheerful babel of voices, among which he thought that he detected 'Erb's. The keys were on the outside of both doors, but he did not turn them. Someone might want to leave on an errand and he had no need to lock in the staff until his job was done. But he slipped along to the outer door of the servants' quarters, and extracted its key, which he dropped among the logs in a basket which stood outside the wine cellar.

There was a clock in the passage which led to the main rooms of the house, and its hands pointed to twenty minutes past nine. The servants must finish their meal by a quarter to ten if Mr. Blett and the footmen were to be ready for dinner. That meant that Bill had under half an hour for his job, which was none too much.

His first business was to visit the butler's pantry to see what champagne remained there. There were only two cases, for the contents of the others were now in the dining-room. Bill tiptoed along the corridor, past the connecting door, which he locked behind him, and entered the dining-room by way of the central hall. From the bedrooms upstairs came the sound of laughter and human speech, but all the lower part of the house was very quiet. The silence was broken only by the crackling of logs in the great hall fireplace.

Bill's heart almost failed him when he snapped the switch and the blue and crimson lights blazed from the eerie walls. This was a horrible place, and it needed all his resolution to quell his tremors. . . . But presently he was too busy to be afraid. Somehow or other he had to shift several dozen bottles, and he looked round for a means of transport. He found it in a dumb-waiter from which the upper tray could be removed. This he loaded carefully with wine and then wished himself in the Wild-ash schoolroom.

This was a very humble scene compared with the uncanny grandeur he had left. There was a trestle table covered with a rather ragged oil-cloth, and on it stood several loaves, a dish of butter, a wedge of cheap cheese, some odd-looking plates of meat, and four big brown earthenware jugs of beer. A small fire burned in the grate, and a feeble oil lamp revealed the dingy walls with their ancient oleographs of royalties. Altogether the scene of the Pig Club supper did not suggest revelry.

Bill arranged the champagne bottles on the table and twirled the stick. . . . The Hall dining-room was as he had left it. Three times the tray was loaded up and transferred to the schoolroom, till there was not a bottle of any sort left behind. Champagne, brandy, liqueurs of many brands, and three decanters of port were now making a brave show on the school-room oilcloth. Then he transported the two cases of champagne remaining in the butler's pantry. And then he paused for a moment to think. The clock on the mantelpiece said 9.30.

He had intended only to take the wine. But the recollection of the Pig Club's meagre fare suggested an amendment to his plan. He would give them some of the eatables also. So the tray was loaded with Strassburg patés, and game-pies, and hams and tongues and galantines, and a basket of hot-house fruits ; and to crown all a cake so rich that Bill's mouth watered at the sight of it. But he realised that he must take nothing for himself, or *Bands* would have something to say about it. He was no brigand, but a minister of justice.

The transfer of these delicacies took a full ten minutes. Bill, now back in the dining-room, turned off the lights, for the fire gave enough illumination. There was very little solid fare left in that place, and absolutely nothing to drink. No doubt hot dishes would be forthcoming from the kitchen, but the Benisons must make shift without champagne. He did not touch a variety of comfits and sweet dishes, for he remembered that the Wildash Pig Club were simple souls and would make little of such dainties.

He listened, and heard a clock far away strike the three-quarters. Soon there would be movement in the servants' region, though he had made it impossible for them to reach the dining-room, since he had hidden the key. But the guests seemed to be astir, for he heard steps in the hall. He was just about to take his leave when the door opened.

Bill, crouching behind the table, lingered spell-bound. The newcomer was a tall man, and he was dressed to resemble an African witch-doctor—at least, after the first moment of scare, this was Bill's verdict. He had horns on his head and a necklace of bones round his neck, his face was horribly painted in white and red, and he seemed to be naked except for a loin cloth of skins. He closed the door very softly behind him and made no attempt to turn on the lights. Evidently he knew his way, for he advanced to the sideboard. Bill decided that he was suffering from a great thirst.

Now Bill had pulled out the biggest wine-cooler from below that sideboard in order to extract the bottles, and he had not pushed it back. The visitor was feeling along the sideboard top with his face to the door, and, oblivious of his danger, he took a step backwards. In a moment an African witch-doctor was sitting in six inches of ice and water, wailing like a sea-bird.

Bill waited no longer. This was an un-rehearsed effect, but it was proof that the fates recognised the justice of his enterprise.

The fire in the schoolroom was burning a little more cheerfully. Bill turned up the lamp to contemplate his handiwork. The trestle table groaned under its load of rich provender, and the bottles made a shining forest about it. The shabby oilcloth was completely hidden by them, and the shabbier tin plates and broken-handled knives. Bill stirred the fire, and set all the chairs he could find in order round the board. At the far end of the room the school benches had been piled, and these made a screen behind which he ensconced himself. He wanted to see the expression on the faces of the first arrivals.

He was disappointed. The Wildash Pig Club were men of iron, immune from nerves and very willing to accept the gifts of a mysterious Providence. When they lumbered in, with the slow step of those who have been labouring hard all day, and the glory was revealed to them, Pobjoy rose to the occasion. He ceremoniously locked the door. Then he sat down in the

THAT PIG CLUB SUPPER WAS TO REMAIN A HALLOWED MEMORY, NOT
IN WILDASH ALONE, BUT IN ALL THE SEVEN TOWNS OF ALEMOOR.

p. 83

presidential chair and said grace huskily. Then
he demanded a corkscrew.

That Pig Club supper was to remain a
hallowed memory, not in Wildash alone, but in
all the Seven Towns of Alemoor. They drank
up all the champagne, but not neat, for neat it
seemed to them to be but a cold and comfortless
beverage. With the beer they made a new
shandygaff, and with brandy and liqueurs they
concocted heart-stirring mixtures, worthy to
wash down food which was a heavenly revela-
tion. Instead of the low mutter of casual talk
which commonly attended the supper, they
soared into Bacchanalian happiness. They
drank each other's healths with due honours,
and the Wardsley keeper proposed the toast of
Pobjoy, whose poaching instincts he had hitherto distrusted, dwelling eloquently on his talents
as a sportsman and his worth as a citizen.
Repeatedly they honoured the memory of old
Squire John, with whom they somehow connected their good fortune. Men who had not
sung since their schooldays were moved to
melody.

They did not return soberly to their wives at
midnight, as had been their custom. The
school-mistress next door was kept awake by

their revelry far into the small hours. When, just before dawn, they emerged into a snowy world, the sharp air turned even those seasoned vessels into madcaps. Springwell, the thatcher, was found by the Vicar before the morning service asleep in the church porch, and Noggin the blacksmith was discovered in his own smithy with his head on a heap of iron filings. The Coldeaston shepherd was, after much searching, disinterred from a hay shed many miles distant from his dwelling, while Martin the ditcher having safely reached his cottage, was so ill-inspired as to don his morris-dancer's clothes and caper in the village street to the accompaniment of the village church bells.

Pobjoy alone was unshaken. He marched steadily home, announcing to the world that the fly was on the turnip and that he preferred turnip-hoeing to any other earthly occupation. But even Pobjoy wept happily for some time on Jum's neck.

CHAPTER NINE

THE ADVENTURE OF UNCLE BOB—I

BILL was snug in bed before his mother appeared at eleven o'clock to fill his stocking. He put up a very good imitation of healthful slumber, and fortunately she did not notice the heap of wet clothing tumbled in a corner. When she had gone, he rose and so disposed of that clothing that it should not catch the eye of Elsie in the morning.

Christmas dawned upon a white world. Bill was wakened by an excited Peter displaying the treasures of his stocking, and lay for a little trying to reconstruct the events of the past evening. He waited eagerly to hear the news of them—eagerly, but with a little anxiety too. All had gone according to plan, but there were the after-effects to reckon with. The simple course would have been to seek out Thomas the keeper, who would be found in the gun-room preparing for the Christmas shoot. But Bill decided that he had better hold himself aloof.

The news must come to him—he must not go to seek it.

So he was a little abstracted at breakfast, though ceremonially grateful for his Christmas gifts and inclined to frown on Peter's extravagances. At church he felt self-conscious. There was no member of the Pig Club there, and he did not know about the Vicar's discovery of the sleeping Springwell in the porch, but he suspected that even the most decorous worshippers must have spent the morning discussing the doings at Wildash.

The killing of the Christmas pheasant in the afternoon was as much a part of the family ritual as church, and Bill, who from his preoccupation with other things, escaped his besetting fault of over-keenness, managed to get five to his own 16-bore. As the birds were being collected he realised that his father was being told a tale by the beaters, and he could scarcely refrain from joining the group. His father's laughter reassured him ; that must mean that there had been no regrettable incident.

The story came out at tea. Bill had never seen his father so amused.

" Best thing I ever heard of ! The Benisons had one of their freak parties last night, and were laying themselves out for a vulgar jamboree. Some genius came along, locked up the servants and pinched all the wine and most of the food. Was there ever a finer case of the biter bit ? Those brutes got some of their own medicine, and I hope they enjoyed it."

"And that's only half the fun," his father continued. "The same good fairy transported the Benisons' provender to the Wildash schoolroom, and the Pig Club, when they arrived for their modest supper, found a feast of fat things. Like sensible fellows they asked no questions, but ate it all up. Drank it all up, too, with the result that the Pig Club to-day seems to be dispersed over the countryside. Old Loveday says that there are still search parties out. . . . I gather they had nothing to do with the plundering of the Benisons—only found the stuff on their supper table and very naturally demolished it. Loveday says that every man-jack of them has a water-tight alibi, and can account for every minute till he arrived at the schoolroom. The Benisons of course are furious, and have turned on the police, but it looks as if they could do nothing. I hope to goodness they don't catch the sportsman who did the trick. I wish I knew who he was, for I'd like to shake hands with him. Hang it all, Mary, the whole country should subscribe to pay his fine, if they catch him, and present him with a piece of plate."

Bill, feeling that some observation was expected from him, enquired if Thomas the keeper had attended the supper.

" Thomas was there," said his father. " He was looking a little pink about the gills this afternoon, and drank a lot of water. When I spoke to him he only grinned, for with the police court in view Thomas is not going to give himself away. But I seemed to detect a holy joy in his eyes."

The period between tea and dinner on Christmas Day was by custom consecrated to reading aloud in the library. Bill scarcely listened to the stirring tale of Jim Hawkins, for his soul was bubbling with satisfaction. He had brought off a feat for which his father thought a piece of plate a fitting recognition. He had executed justice upon the disturbers of the local peace. He had given a number of honest men the high moment of their lives. . . .

But one obstinate question remained to disturb his mind. He was not yet clear whether his staff was *Beauty* or *Bands*, and till he had settled that problem he could have no true confidence. Last night's escapade had been a suitable task for either.

When his mother and Barbara had gone up to dress Bill was left alone for a few minutes with his father. Now was the chance to see if any enlightenment could be got from the old book. He plunged boldly into the subject, and asked for more of the tale he had been told three nights before. His father got down the folio and looked up the passage.

" There isn't much more here," he said. " You see, the writer is dealing with St. Egbert's contests with the Devil, and only brings in the *Beauty* and *Bands* story as an illustration."

" Did the magic staff play tricks with people if they used it wrongly ? I mean, did it take them to some queer place and then refuse to work, or anything like that ? "

" I don't think so. The staff wasn't mischievous, even if *Bands* was mistaken for *Beauty* or *Beauty* for *Bands*. So far as I can make out, if it was offended it merely took the huff and quietly disappeared. That must be so—if it had been otherwise this old fellow would have had something to say about the staff putting its owner in the cart. That's just the kind of yarn he would have loved."

Bill went up to dress with his mind at ease.

After dinner they all listened to the news on

the wireless, for they had a strong family interest in it. Bill's uncle Bob, his mother's only brother, had been a distinguished airman in the War, and was now a great swell in civil aviation. He had made several record flights, and was at present attempting to fly alone to the Cape and back in a new type of light plane. So far he had done brilliantly. He had lowered the time for the outward journey by fourteen hours, and was already more than half-way home. He had left Kano in Northern Nigeria that morning, said the wireless, and was expected to reach the Mediterranean coast that evening. To-morrow he was due to arrive in England and preparations were being made to give him a public welcome. To Bill, who deeply admired his uncle, the news was the coping stone to a joyous day, and he went to bed in high spirits.

But alas ! next morning came a different story. His mother appeared at breakfast with a white face and eyes that looked as if she had been crying. The papers had come, and there in large type it was written that Captain Robert Askew had not reached the coast. Bill's father had already telephoned to London and found that the report was true. Uncle Bob and his plane had simply vanished. Twelve hours earlier he should have been in Algiers, but there

was no sign of him. The French air posts had
been warned, but the Sahara is a biggish area in
which to look for a small plane, and Uncle Bob
had no wireless attachment. The fear was that
he had developed engine trouble somewhere
among those inhospitable sands, and had been
forced down. If he could not ascend again, he
was lost—lost, maybe, for weeks—and would
probably perish. The trouble was that he had
not chosen to inform anyone about the exact
course he meant to take, so he had left no data
for a rescue party to work on.

Breakfast was a silent meal. Bill wept a
little out of sympathy with his mother, and then
went out into the garden to think.

The weather had grown mild again, the snow
had disappeared, and the first aconites were
showing below the trees in the rookery. But
Bill had no eyes for the garden ; he was seeing
an infinite solitude of yellow desert with a small
disconsolate object in the midst of it. He was
very fond of Uncle Bob, and it was borne in on
him that if he did not do something he might
never see Uncle Bob again. This was a different
kind of adventure from any he had engaged in
before ; it was desperately serious, since life
was at stake, and because it was so serious he
was afraid.

But he saw no other way. If he failed Uncle Bob in his peril he would be ashamed of himself all his life. . . . It would be a longish business, and he must make some excuse and get off for the day. Happily he was quit of Peter, who was in bed with a violent cold in his head ; even in the garden the horns of elfland faintly blown announced that Peter was doing good work with a pocket handkerchief. Bill got the cook to cut him some sandwiches, and then sought out his mother and announced that he wanted to go for a long walk.

" That's a wise child," said his father. " The best cure for anxiety is to stretch your legs. Perhaps we may have better news when you get home."

His mother kissed the top of his head. She looked so pale and sad that Bill's reluctant resolution kindled into a crusading zeal.

CHAPTER TEN

THE ADVENTURE OF UNCLE BOB—II

IN a glade of a wood about two miles from home, Bill twirled his stick and wished himself with his uncle. . . .

He found himself in a place very unlike the foggy morning Midlands he had left. It was cold, colder than at home, the sky was the palest blue, and his own shadow was long on the little hills. Funny hummocky little hills they were, like sand ridges on the seashore shaped into fantastic patterns by the tide. On the top of one of them sat a man with his chin in his right hand, looking towards the east, where a great golden sun was climbing the heavens.

" Uncle Bob," said Bill.

The man, who was dressed in rough overalls, did not turn his head.

" Uncle Bob," said Bill again.

This time the head moved round and Bill saw a drawn white face with hollow eyes, very different from the robust Uncle Bob he remembered. Apparently the man's eyes were

less incredulous than his ears, for at the sight
of Bill he jumped to his feet.

"Good God!" he cried, "this is serious.
My eyes have gone." He rubbed them and
peered wildly at the small boy in front of him.

Bill was scared by his reception. "Uncle
Bob," he cried, "don't look like that. It's me.
It's really me."

"Who are you?" The voice was as wild as
the eyes.

"Me! Bill! I've come to help you."

The man groaned and dropped on the grass.
"Lord," he moaned, "this is the end of things.
I'm clean off my head."

"You're not. It's really me, Bill!" He
put out his hand and stroked his uncle's
arm.

The man caught him by the shoulder. "Am
I mad or dreaming? No! By Jove, you feel
real. You really are Bill." He sniffed the
sleeve of Bill's jacket. "That's Harris tweed.
You must be real. Where, by all that is marvellous, have you come from?"

"From home."

"But how?"

"It's magic," said Bill. "I can't explain,
but anyhow I'm here. I've come to help you.
The papers this morning said that you might

have crashed, so I came to help you. . . . Will you have a sandwich?"

Uncle Bob took a bite of one of Bill's sandwiches and then sat down again with his head in his hands.

"Great Scott!" he cried. "The papers this morning! And that sandwich was cut less than an hour ago! Either I'm delirious or it's a blessed miracle."

He was on his feet again, pawing and kneading the boy's shoulders as if afraid they would vanish into a mirage.

"You feel solid enough. And you look like Bill. . . . Miracle or no, you're here at this moment beside me in this blighted desert. Come along and I'll show you what has happened."

He seized the boy's arm and raced him across the sand dunes. Bill noticed that Uncle Bob was not very steady on his legs, like a man who was very stiff or very tired. They had not gone more than three hundred yards when they came on a little plane, the new Phantom Gnat which was the apple of Uncle Bob's eye. It did not look like a wreck, for it sat as lightly in that sandy hollow as a mayfly on a stream.

"No, there was no crash," Bill was told. "I made a fair landing, but just in time, for there's bad mischief there. Nothing that a good mechanic with proper spares couldn't put right in twenty minutes. Only, you see, I haven't got the spares—that's my infernal carelessness. As it is, the thing might be scrap-iron for all the use it is to me at present. . . . Man, I was twenty-seven hours ahead of the record when this dashed catastrophe happened. . . . As it is, I'm about twelve hours to the good, if I could get on. Only I can't. I'm absolutely and eternally dished. I might as well be down in the middle of the Atlantic."

The sun was getting hotter and brighter, and the glory of quintessential light made every sandhill shine like polished gold.

" I've food and water enough for a couple of days," Uncle Bob went on. " After that I perish, for there's not much chance of being picked up, and I'll never reach Farakesh." He seemed not to be talking to Bill, but communing with himself.

" Where's Farakesh ? " Bill asked.

Uncle Bob flung a wild arm towards the west.

" Somewhere out there. . . . I took my bearings when I landed, but the maps for this part of the world are no more use than a sick-headache. Farakesh might be fifty miles or it might be a hundred, and on a compass course

I'm not likely to hit it off—let alone the chances against slogging the distance before my supplies gave out. . . . And what about you ? I don't know how you got here, but now you're in the same boat as me, and we're both for it."

" That's all right," said Bill. " Don't worry about me, Uncle Bob. Mother was so sad about you this morning (' This morning ! ' Uncle Bob wailed)—we all were except Peter— that I had to do something. What's Farakesh ? "

" It's a French post . . . Spahis, I believe. I don't think they've any planes there, but they're sure to have Citroëns and mechanics. They could patch me up all right, but I might as well wish for the moon."

Suddenly Bill felt very old, far older than his uncle.

" I want you to write a letter, please," he said. " A letter to the French, saying what you want."

" To be picked up by the postman on his rounds, I suppose ? "

" No. By me," said Bill. " Don't ask questions, Uncle Bob, for I can't explain, but please write the letter. There's no time to waste, if you're to beat the record."

" I'm mad," said Uncle Bob, " undoubtedly

mad," and he put his hands to his head. But he also ferreted about in the plane and produced a pencil and paper. First he wrote a message in English, explaining his whereabouts as well as he could and the nature of the help he wanted. Then below he wrote a French translation. Then he put it in an envelope and addressed it to the Commandant at Farakesh.

" This is like putting a request for help into a bottle and chucking it into the ocean just when you're going to be washed off your raft," he said. " Now, you amazing child, what do you propose to do ? "

" I'm going to Farakesh," said Bill. " Please don't look round. I promise not to be long."

Bill put a sandhill between himself and the plane and twisted his stick. . . . He found himself in a dusty hollow where a string of horses was exercising, with riders who appeared to be dressed in white nightgowns and nightcaps. There was a long, low, white building before him with a dome in the centre. There was also a group of short dusty palm trees, and a pool of dirty green water surrounded by a stone coping, and, on the high ground behind, a jungle of thorns intersected by sandy roads.

That was all that Bill's eyes took in of Fara-

kesh, for he had no time for the study of landscape. He marched up to the entrance where
a sentry was on duty, a man in faded blue
uniform whose rifle carried a queer thin kind
of bayonet.

" *Pour Monsieur le Commandant*," said Bill,
drawing upon his exiguous store of the French
tongue.

The sentry, confronted by a small boy in a
tweed suit of knickerbockers, a tweed cap and
muddy shoes, nearly had a fit. He brought
down the butt of his rifle with a clang on the
stone, and called upon the Virgin and the Saints.
He cried shrilly for his colleagues, and soon
Bill was surrounded by an excited group who
plied him with questions in a French which he
did not understand. Then an officer came along
and the group stood to attention.

He was a very lean officer and he was scarcely
less excited than the sentry. He, too, began a
cross-examination, but Bill could not make anything of his rapid speech and decided that he
had better not try. He only shook his head
and smiled and pointed to the letter.

The officer took him by the hand and led him
indoors through many whitewashed passages to
a room where a little grizzled old man sat at a
table covered with papers. The little old man,

who Bill decided must be the Commandant, had two lines of medal ribbons on his breast.

Then followed a vivacious colloquy. Uncle Bob's letter was opened and read, and more officers were summoned. " It is without doubt the Capitaine Robert Askew," Bill made out that much of the conversation. " But how ? But why ? "

Bill found himself the object of the acutest interest, and he seemed to be referred to as an " *enfant merveilleux.*" He only smiled and nodded.

Maps were eagerly unrolled. They seemed to know where Uncle Bob was, and a spot was marked and calculations made. Bill heard the number " *soixante-dix* " repeated many times and joined to the word " *kilometres.*"

Then the conclave was suddenly broken up. He was taken to a large cool room full of long tables, and given food—a big glass of milk as thick as cream which had an odd lemony taste, the best dates he had ever eaten, and delicious little thin sugar cakes.

Then he was led out into the sunshine, where two long squat motor-cars were waiting, with very broad wheels. There was an officer and a man in each, and an assortment of ironmongery. Bill was packed into the first car, the Commandant to his disgust kissed him on both cheeks, and he was whirled into the glittering desert. But first an officer had twined a long gauzy white cloth round his head, a thing like a turban. Bill realised that a cap suited for an Oxfordshire winter was scarcely adequate in a Sahara noon.

Bill was to remember that journey because of its acute discomfort. Almost at once he felt sick, either because of the bumpy ground or the luncheon he had eaten. Also he was soon horribly afraid, for never man drove like that French driver. They invited jolts which would have smashed most axles, and they coasted gaily along the slopes of hills where nothing but the pace prevented the car from toppling sideways. Bill clutched at his wits and prayed that it would soon be over, and only the memory of Uncle Bob and a lingering scrap of prudence kept him from twisting his stick and vanishing.

By and by they came into deep sand and had to slow down, and Bill's nausea diminished ; and when at the end of four hours they saw a fire of dry scrub on a distant hillock, which Uncle Bob had lit for a mark, he felt his own master again. He was pleased that Uncle Bob had lit the fire, for it showed that he had some confidence in his nephew.

Then there were bowings and handshakings

and a great deal of rapid French, and Uncle Bob and the mechanics were busy with the inside of the engine. A fire was made, a little anvil was set up, and for an hour in that blistering noontide men hammered and screwed and bored. Then the work was over. Uncle Bob climbed into the pilot's seat, and taxied along the sand, and the engine proved to be working sweetly. He got out again and shook hands with the Frenchmen, and they all made him speeches.

Bill, foreseeing the end of his duties, had climbed to the top of one of the dunes. " Good-bye, Uncle Bob, and good luck," he cried, when he saw that all was well.

Uncle Bob, reawakened to his nephew's presence, exclaimed and began to run towards him. So did the Frenchmen. " Bill ! " he called. " Come here, Bill ! " and the others shouted about a miraculous child.

But Bill felt that further intercourse would be embarrassing. He nipped down the far side of the dune and twirled his stick. . . .

He was standing in Elder's Spinney on sodden turf, while a fine rain was filtering through the beeches. The sand of the Sahara was in the crinkles of his shoes and knickerbockers and in the corners of his eyes. When he had gone half a mile he suddenly remembered that he was still wearing the turban which had been given him at Farakesh. This he removed and stuffed into a rabbit hole.

That evening at tea he told the family that there was a rumour in the village that Uncle Bob was all right, but he was not believed till the wireless confirmed the news. Next morning a late edition of an enterprising penny paper announced the safe arrival of Captain Askew at Croydon, and his reception by the Under-Secretary for Air. He had broken the record by eight hours.

CHAPTER ELEVEN

THE ADVENTURE OF THE IVORY VALLEY—I

THE news of Uncle Bob's success put Bill into a state of high exaltation. He felt proud of himself, for, though he owed his achievement to the magic stick, he had surely shown boldness in his use of it.

It was one of those hopeless days which mid-winter brings to the English Midlands. Rain fell with a dull persistency, and an east wind swirled round the manor gables, coming through the gap between the rookery and the tithe barn. Bill did not suffer much from cold, but he loved bright weather, and he felt himself homesick for yesterday's riot of sunlight. Also he hungered for more of Africa. He had been in the Solomon Islands, and had seen there one of the countries of his dreams. He had smelt the hot drought of the Sahara and looked over its yellow distances. What he wanted now to round off his experiences was a tropical forest.

Peter was bed-ridden with his cold, and after

breakfast Bill sat himself by the library fire. He had the day before him, and, since it was his family's habit to disregard weather, he would be allowed to go off with sandwiches in his pocket to try for snipe on the fringes of Alemoor. But Alemoor was not for him. He wanted colour and light and mystery.

He was a great devourer of travel books, and could have reeled off the names of many out-landish places. Central Africa had always been one of his fancies, partly because his father as a young man had gone there after big game. Bill remembered his father's tales—how he had looked at the summit of the Mountains of the Moon from a hundred miles off and thought it a thunder-cloud—how he had first seen the silver cone of Kilimanjaro while lost in the waterless bush—how he had pushed inside the fringes of the dark Congo forest. Certain names—Ruwenzori, Tanganyika, Ruanda—sang in Bill's head like tunes.

But especially he remembered one of his father's tales which an old hunter had told him in Mozambique. He was a grizzled old man called Stubber, and he had a withered leg which a lion had once chawed. He had been a famous elephant-hunter in his day, and this was his story.

Somewhere in the mountains was a valley where the elephants went when they felt death approaching. They had done this for thousands of years, and the place was full of ivory—such tusks as no hunter had ever looked on. The way to it was hard to find, and Stubber had never been there himself, though he had often tried to reach it. One or two men had looked at the valley from the neighbouring ridges, but had not been able to make their way back to it.

But let a bold man go there, said Stubber, and let him blaze a trail for transport, and he had in his hand the fortune of kings. For, said he, diamonds are going down in price, and gold isn't what it was, but fine ivory will have its market till the crack of doom.

Bill had no commercial ambitions. *Bands* would not allow that. He got out the big atlas and poured over a map of equatorial Africa. His father had not been very clear which mountains Stubber had meant, for the old fellow had been so drunk for a week after the tale that he could get no more out of him. There seemed to be a good many mountain ranges—Rudolf, Kenya, Kilimanjaro, Ruwenzori, and a lot of volcanoes. His father had said that if he had had more time during his hunting trip he would have had a shot at finding the Ivory Valley.

Why, Bill asked himself, should he not take on the job ? Stubber had been vague, but the magic staff would know all about it.

Bill looked out of the library window and watched the rain drifting over the lawn. He felt a great longing for Africa. Without more ado he went up to his bedroom and got into flannel shorts and a thin shirt ; then he put on his thickest overcoat and announced to his mother that he was going out for the day.

She made no objection.

" I'm glad you are taking your ulster with you," she said, " for it is very cold, and you are usually rather naughty about wrapping up. Don't be a minute later than four o'clock in getting back. The Harding children are coming to tea, and Peter is in bed, so you will have to be a good boy and help to entertain them."

As Bill dived into the thick cover of Wildash Great Spinney he thought with amusement of the Harding children. Two foolish little pig-tailed girls ! He hid his gun and his overcoat among the bracken and stood up to twirl the stick in clothes fit only for the hottest July afternoon.

His first thought was that the staff had misunderstood him. He had pictured a valley like a Highland glen, a bright open place with a tumbling burn in the midst of it. Instead he found himself in a cavern.

It was an enormous cavern, at least half a mile broad and a mile or two long. It was dark, the sun being not yet high enough to enter it, but Bill saw far above him a band of deep violet sky. On all sides were sheer walls of rock, black as coal at the foot, but showing a faint pink towards the summit. Never had he seen, never had he dreamed of, such tremendous precipices. Even a bird would be weary before it surmounted them.

The floor of the valley seemed to be sand and rock, and there was no stream. Indeed, the intense dryness of the place was what first struck him, far drier than the Sahara of yesterday. His mouth seemed in a moment to grow hot and his lips to grow hard, while he felt an odd difficulty in drawing breath.

But the main thing was the stench. It was awful—a combination of all the worst smells that Bill ever remembered. It afflicted him like a toothache ; also he felt giddy and a little sick. He sat down, and presently jumped up, for on the ground there was something—something rotting and horrible.

It took all his fortitude to carry on. Holding his nose he looked round him. He was close to the lower end of the valley, and the ground was piled with gruesome shapes—heaps of grey, dust-covered skin, which had split in parts and showed awful blue decomposing flesh. Out of these masses stuck yellow tusks like the bowsprits of ships. He was in a graveyard, an open graveyard, where the corpses of great beasts lay like pebbles on a beach.

He could not stay there, for he was retching with nausea, and he was in terror of fainting and falling down among these horrid relics. He must move, for a little way ahead he thought he saw what looked like barer ground strewn with whitish-grey stones. So he ran, stumbling, picking his way among the rotting masses, and now and then slipping on some slimy horror. With one hand holding his nose and the other clutching his stick, he managed to get out of the lower trough of the valley to a higher level.

Here the stench began to abate, and in its place came a dry, half-sweet smell, like that of an old calf-bound book, or the vaults of the village church when summer abated their damp. He realised the meaning of it all. In the lower end of the valley were the elephants that had come there recently to die, but he was now moving towards the relics of ancient death.

It was a marvellous place in which he found himself. The sun was getting up in the heavens and about half of one side of the rocks was a rosy gold. The light was now clear enough to reveal the whole extent of the valley. Bill found himself walking in a place exactly like a seashore—only instead of sand there was a fine grey dust, into which myriads of dead elephants had crumbled. Everywhere, piled and scattered at random, were things like the ribs of old shipwrecked boats.

Such tusks he had never dreamed of. Some were like the jaw-bones of whales which he remembered seeing at coast villages in Scotland. They were black with age, but when he scraped with his penknife he revealed the white ivory beneath. Some had got a dull yellow colour with queer red ochreous stains. It was the size of them more than their number that amazed him, and then he knew the reason. The elephants who came here to die must have been the kings of the herd, the finest and strongest, who could escape their enemies of the forest and find a natural death of old age.

He could breathe freely now, though there

was still that dryness in his throat which made him cough. He had no longer any repulsion towards the things at his feet. They seemed to him natural and harmless, like the horns of deer which hung in the hall and corridors at home.

As he picked his way through the dust he felt very solemn. He was the first mortal that had ever entered this sepulchre. Many had tried for it and fought their way up through the desert and jungles, but none had ever trod this floor. The thought did not make Bill exult. He felt very much as he had felt in church the week before when he attended old Grampound's funeral.

And then suddenly his mood changed. He looked up at the beetling walls and felt himself choking ; he was alone here in this pit of death, a prisoner in a tomb.

Bill was not much afraid of ghosts, and this bare silent place was not ghostly, for it had no connection with human life. But he felt what, if he had known it, the Greeks called " panic," the terror of man in the face of a nature which he has not subdued.

He felt his heart fluttering and something moving in his throat which stopped his breath. For a second his eyes dazzled and he almost fainted. Then an overpowering desire came upon him to escape, and with that desire a little clearness of mind.

He twirled the staff and wished himself on the top of the cliffs, on the containing rim of the valley.

CHAPTER TWELVE

THE ADVENTURE OF THE IVORY VALLEY—II

IT was suddenly quite cool, and Bill breathed pleasantly again.

He looked back, and there beneath him —miles beneath him it seemed, like a landscape seen through the wrong end of a telescope—was the Ivory Valley. From the height on which he stood it was so distant that the bottom seemed only a blur of grey, like the floor of the sea when you look down from a boat through deep waters. No one standing on that ridge could realise what lay at the foot of the sword-cut. How did the dying beasts enter ?—that was what puzzled Bill.

It was a very wonderful place. At the head of the valley was a huge moraine, and beyond it a glistening cap of snow. There were the shoulders and summits of other mountains in the same direction, which Bill realised was the west. But to east and north a blue plain ran out to the horizon, a plain with a shimmering haze in the far distance. It must have been very far below him, for in the foreground wave after wave of foot-hills descended to it like a cascade.

Not only the view but the air told Bill how high up he was. It would have been chilly, but for the glare of the sun which wrapped him round like a warm bath. Bill's tweed cap was not much of a protection, so he used his handkerchief to screen his neck.

Then he took note of his immediate surroundings. He dare not look back into the depths of the valley, so he turned to the flat rim of it. There was turf here very like Scotland, short mossy turf, with wonderful little flowers. But a few yards from the edge a covert began. Bill called it a covert to himself, for it should have been a covert, but it was magnified to the dimensions of a forest.

There was heather, real heather, but it grew as tall as birch trees. There was bracken of a most miraculous size. There were what looked like groundsels, but they had become as big as oaks. It was as if a bit of Scots moorland had been swollen into a garden for giants. And there was everywhere a delicious aromatic fragrance.

But what concerned Bill was the geography

of the Ivory Valley. How did the elephants enter ? He felt all the zest of the explorer on the edge of a mighty secret. Clearly not at the top, for there was no inlet by the way of the snow mountain. Not by the sides, for nothing could descend those glassy rock walls. It must be by the foot. Now Bill judged that he was not more than a mile from the foot, so he started off to prospect along the rim.

For the sake of shade he dived into the covert, emerging only when the bracken grew too much for him. There were birds in plenty—one looking very like a blackbird with a scarlet breast ; and a kind of finch which piped divinely. Also there was a multitude of bright moths, a subject of which Bill knew nothing. But there was no sign of anything dangerous, though Bill went circumspectly, for he remembered his father's tales of mambas and fierce bush-buck rams and crouching leopards.

Presently he was forced back on to the scarp, which had changed its character. The turf was gone and the wildwood had crept up and covered it. He made his way to the edge in quest of a view. He was very near the bottom end of the valley—that much he realised, but he could not make out any way of entrance.

A few yards more and he discovered it. There

was a rift in the containing wall, for the ground seemed to sink under his feet. He looked down over tree-tops to a V-shaped gap far below him.

It seemed possible to descend, and Bill, after a moment's hesitation, started out. The angle was steep, but not too steep to prevent trees finding a footing, and it was through a clinging forest that Bill made his way. He began by slithering down a long bank of earth and stones which scarified his bare legs. After that he grew bold and took big leaps, calculating to stop himself by the trees. In this way he descended about half the distance into the gap.

Then the character of the wood changed. The whole hillside seemed to ooze water. Every few yards was a spring and the ground was seamed with tiny watercourses. With the water came a different vegetation. The wood took on a new character, for it was thicker, wilder, greener, and desperately tangled. Asparagus creepers began to festoon the trees, and bright flowers of a species quite unknown to Bill clothed the sides of each runnel. Also there were thorns, long trailing things which almost tore the shirt and shorts from his body. It had become very hot, and the sweat clouded his eyes.

Still he descended, rolling, slipping, jumping,

until he came to a covert so thick that he had to crawl with his face almost in the mud. This was the place for a tiger-cat or a bush-buck ram, and the thought made Bill increase his speed. He was determined to get to the gap, but he held himself ready at any moment to twirl the staff.

The jungle ceased and Bill finished his course on a smooth slope of screes. He finished it dramatically, for he rolled the last hundred feet and stood up breathless to look about him.

It was a pass sure enough, the entry into the Ivory Valley. Behind on the forest side was a long descending gulley, rolled smooth like an alley in a pine wood along which trees have been drawn. By this path the dying elephants had ascended from all Equatoria.

On the valley side there was also a slope, but far steeper and sheerer. It was rubbed bare of both vegetation and stones, a long shoot of earth ending up among fallen boulders. Bill rubbed his eyes and saw that they were not boulders, but the rotting carcases he had already visited. It was like a gigantic toboggan run, and the elephants, when they wearily reached the pass, must have, with their last strength, glissaded into their sepulchre.

Very still and solemn was Bill as he looked at this portal of death. Then a little way up on the left-hand side something caught his eye. It was a bare place, a rocky shelf, and something white lay on it.

He saw that it was bones, and something told him that they were human. This had been the last camp of a pioneer who had found the valley only to die. Long ago the bones had been picked clean by bird and beast, and were now only to be distinguished by their blanched whiteness from the grey screes.

There was something more there. Bill picked out of the stones five coins. They were discoloured and encrusted, but gold beyond doubt. He rubbed them and one showed a king's head on it, and another some spidery marks like Chinese letters. The dead adventurer must have belonged to a very distant generation.

Bill pocketed them. This was not loot, he felt, but a legitimate find, and *Bands* could not disapprove.

And then across the gap he saw that which put everything else out of his head. It was not a bush-buck ram or a leopard, but something far more formidable. A huge animal had come out of the covert. At first Bill thought it was a savage, for it squatted on its heels like a human being and beat its breast with its arms ; also from its mouth came a dreadful throaty muttering, like that of some madman in a nightmare.

The gorilla brooded like some obscene vampire that drew its life from this place of death. It had caught sight of Bill and was staring at him with red eyes. Then its muttering changed into a howl of rage. With one mighty bound it covered half the distance between them.

Bill did not stay upon the order of his going.

He sat in the dripping silence of Wildash Great Spinney for a full five minutes before the terrible sound had gone out of his ears. He felt very much shaken and solemnised, and also very cold. He was glad of his overcoat.

" La, Master Bill ! " Elsie the nurse exclaimed when she saw him. " What have you done to your clothes ? You look as if you had been clawed by a gorilla." In high dudgeon she removed the ragged remains of his shirt and breeches.

Bill behaved very well at tea. He was quiet and gentle, and played most amiably with the Harding children. He was glad to be back among the kindly faces of the living, even if they were pig-tailed little girls. He locked the five gold coins in his money-box, for they rather frightened him.

CHAPTER THIRTEEN

BILL HEARS OF PRINCE ANATOLE

THERE was still a fortnight before the holidays ended, and to the employment of this space of time Bill addressed himself like a usurer. The position was not without difficulties.

First there was Peter. Bill had decided that the discretion of that gay youth was not to be trusted. He could not be admitted further into the game, for his twittering nerves would certainly betray it. The Glenmore visit had convinced Bill of that, for with the utmost difficulty Peter had been prevented from blabbing the whole story next morning at breakfast. Threats were of no use, physical violence was futile, and the only way was to convince Peter that the adventure had been a dream. At Peter's age one is not an exact reasoner, and he had come to accept this view, especially as Bill had laid himself out to be especially kind to him, and he did not feel in the mood to contradict a beneficent brother.

Nevertheless, Peter remained a snag. He was devoted to Bill and usually shared most of his holiday enterprises. But with Peter dogging his heels Bill could have no leisure for the magic staff, for he was resolute not to take Peter with him on any further adventures. Yet Bill's heart smote him. Peter was a good little chap and would have a dull time of it if Bill immured himself all day in the recesses of Alemoor. Besides, the family would ask questions—particularly Barbara, who was Peter's special protector.

Then there was Uncle Bob. He was being entertained at some big dinner in London, and must remain in town for several days; but he had wired at once, in reply to the family's congratulations, offering a visit the following week. He said he wanted to see them all again, especially Bill. At any other time these words would have made Bill carry his head high, but now they only embarrassed him.

For Uncle Bob's appearance would be awkward. He was certain to tell the story of Bill's miraculous appearance and heroic conduct. And what was Bill to say? He could of course deny it, but he had a dislike of telling lies, and he knew that he was not very good at it. As a matter of fact, Uncle Bob had decided that the whole episode had been a light-headed dream which inexplicably his French rescuers had shared. He was hopelessly puzzled, but any other conclusion would have meant that he had lost his reason. He only wanted to see Bill to make sure that he had not become a disembodied spirit. But a small boy is not, like his elders, under the bondage of a narrow reason. Bill was convinced that Uncle Bob must regard his visit as a real, if inexplicable, event, and be set on making enquiries.

A way out appeared just before New Year. At breakfast one morning his mother had two announcements to make. Peter and Barbara had been asked to stay for a week with Aunt Alice in London. Barbara was joyful, and Peter, who had a taste for the pleasures of the metropolis, was not unwilling, especially as Aunt Alice was under bond to present him some day with a new camera, and he hoped to expedite the gift.

" Bill, dear," his mother added, " don't you think it would be nice if you paid a visit to Grannie ? You haven't been to see her for nearly a year, and she is getting pretty old, and she is so fond of you."

She expected a protest, for visits to Grannie were not very popular with Bill. Grannie herself was an admitted darling, but she was very old, and very deaf, and very blind, and she did not get out of bed until the afternoon. She had a very old butler called Backus, who was rather cross, and an old maid called Grimes, who was very cross, and an old lame cook, with whom one could not take liberties, and an old head-housemaid who wore spectacles. The house, which was called Farover, was in a dull part of the next county, and there was little for a boy to do there. There was no shooting ; if it froze hard there was no water near to skate on ; there were no ponies ; and there was nobody to play with except the parson's son, a red-headed urchin whom Bill detested.

But to his mother's surprise Bill made no protest. He said meekly that he would rather like to see Grannie again, and that he did not mind if he went to Farover for a bit. His mother was so astounded by this renouncement of the habits of a lifetime that she asked anxiously if he was quite well. Little she knew the sudden exultation in her son's heart.

For things had turned out unbelievably well. Peter was satisfactorily disposed of. The difficult meeting with Uncle Bob was prevented, and Farover would give him just that haunt of ancient peace which he needed. At Farover there was no one to question your doings, for no one was much interested in them. So long as you appeared duly at meals you might spend the intervening hours ranging the earth on a broom-stick.

So it was arranged that the car should deposit Bill at Farover the following evening after tea. Bill sequestered himself in the nursery and gave himself up to the study of a cutting which he had clipped from a picture paper much favoured by Barbara. It was all about a certain Prince Anatole.

Bill had one peculiarity which is important for this tale. Every boy, apart from whatever success he may attain in games or books, is certain to have one hobby in which he is a master—in which, indeed, he absorbs knowledge unconsciously rather than acquires it. One will know everything that is to be known about the rigs of ships, another be a specialist on loco-motives, a third on automobiles, a fourth on birds' nests, others on cricket averages, railway speeds, or athletic records.

Most of Bill's friends were worshippers of speed, either in machines or in human beings. They knew all about speed-boats, and aero-planes, and racing cars, and rapid people like

Chicago gun-men. From the cinema, the press, and popular romances they had equipped themselves with a profound knowledge of the ways of racketeers and hi-jackers and " bad men " generally.

For such things Bill cared not at all. His imagination ranged in more ancient pastures, and he was pre-eminently a child of the Old World. He revelled in history, and in modern life he liked what carried on the pageant of history—courts and castles and turret stairs, secret doors opening on dark lakes, dim cities of the East and crumbling palaces. Bill would not have crossed the street to look at the most notorious gangster, but he would have welcomed the spectacle of a Usurper, a Pretender, or a King in Exile. Chicago said nothing to him, but Samarkand and Stamboul said much. From some mysterious cause the Balkans were for him a name to conjure with. I think the reason was that he had once read in a book that there was always trouble in the Balkans in the spring.

Now the column he had clipped from Barbara's paper contained some fascinating news about the Balkan kingdom of Gracia. It was a very unhappy kingdom, for it could not make up its mind what kind of government it wanted. The House of Paleologue was on the throne, but King Nicholas the Fifth was very old and nearly witless, and the power was in the hands of an ambitious Prime Minister called Kuno, who was believed to fancy himself as head of a Grach republic. Kuno was of peasant origin and had been a good soldier in the war, in which Gracia had suffered heavily from both sides.

King Nicholas had no children alive, and his heir was his grandson, Prince Anatole, a boy of fourteen. According to Barbara's paper, the young Prince's life was a difficult one. He was not allowed to live with his grandfather in the capital city of Grachovo, but was immured in the castle of Mamizan, forty miles off in the mountains. The Grachs were a proud people, but they were also hot-headed and fickle, and Kuno seemed to have convinced them that they could not go on with a demented King. A republic would have been certain but for Prince Anatole, for there was a considerable loyalist party which adhered to him. If the boy could be got out of the road then Kuno's ambitions would certainly be fulfilled.

This story took a strong grip on Bill's mind. Here was a boy only a year older than himself who was the centre of desperate plots, and whose

life must be in hourly danger. Bill had a pre-
ference for monarchy and wanted Anatole to
win. But he felt that the odds were against
him, a prisoner in a lonely castle, with Kuno's
guards clanking their rifles at the gate.

The more he thought about the situation the
less he liked it. The figure of that solitary child
hag-rode his fancy and gave him no peace.
Something must be done about it, and done at
once. He remembered the horrid stories of
King John and Prince Arthur, and the murdered
princes in the Tower.

All the way to Farover Bill meditated pro-
foundly. He arrived at half-past six, and, after
greeting his grandmother, was shown his bedroom by the cross butler, and given supper
in what had once been the nursery. Bill
announced that he was sleepy and meant to go
to bed early. So he was left by Backus reading
beside his bedroom fire, after strict instructions
as to how to turn off the electric light.

Bill did not go to bed. Instead he put on a
sweater over his waistcoat, for he thought that a
Balkan castle in the mountains might be cold.
Then a little nervously, but with the sense that
he was embarking on the high seas of romance,
he twirled the stick and wished himself with
Prince Anatole in Mamizan.

CHAPTER FOURTEEN

THE FIRST ADVENTURE OF MAMIZAN

HE found himself on a slippery roof which was edged by low battlements. It was pitch-dark and an icy wind cut through Bill's clothes, sweater and all, and froze the marrow in his bones. He took a step and promptly sat down hard, and slithered until he was brought up by the parapet. There was no sound except the surge of the wind among the gables, the roar of an adjacent stream, and the melancholy hooting of a great owl.

Bill was horribly scared. Had the magic staff made some awful mistake?

Then he heard another noise, which seemed to be human. Someone close to him was weeping—gulping, at any rate, to choke down tears. Bill felt his nerves steady.

"Hist!" he cried. "Is there anybody there?"

He got to his feet, put out his hand and touched something solid but soft. It was so dark that he could distinguish only a lump of deeper blackness, and from that lump the sound

HE PUT OUT HIS HAND AND TOUCHED SOMETHING SOLID BUT SOFT.

p. 128

came. Yes, beyond doubt, it was sobbing. Somebody was crouching there in dire trouble.

Bill screwed up his courage and poked at the lump. That produced developments. The dark mass straightened itself, and even in the blackness Bill saw that it was a small human figure.

It was a human figure in a panic, for its next move seemed to be to try to escape. It shuffled and sprawled away from Bill, and it suffered Bill's fate, for it slipped upon the steep tiles and was brought up in a heap against the parapet.

To realise that someone is afraid of you is a wonderful cure for your own fears. Bill felt suddenly quite brave and calm.

" Here ! stop ! " he shouted against the wind. " Don't run away. I won't do you any harm."

For a minute no sound of movement came from the huddled figure. Then a voice energed from it, a small broken voice, which was just loud enough for Bill to hear.

" English ! " it said. " It speaks English. Is it a ghost ? "

" It's me," said Bill, " and I'm not a ghost. I've come to help you. Don't scurry off again or you'll make me break my neck. You can feel me and see that I'm real enough."

He crawled along the gutter till he could touch the other. He found his hand and brought it to his cheek—an icy little hand.

" Touch my face," he said, " and you will see that I'm not a ghost. I'm English. I've come to help you."

Then Bill remembered that in his pocket he had an electric torch, a Christmas present from Peter. He pressed the catch and made a tiny circle of light in the darkness. This revealed a boy of little more than his own age, with black hair and pale dirty cheeks. He was dressed in clothes far too small for him, and he had torn a great rent in his breeches. His feet and legs were bare and blue with cold, and one of his toes was bleeding. He looked miserably ill-clad for the place and the weather, for compared with his garb Bill's was like a Polar explorer's.

" You are Prince Anatole, aren't you ? " said Bill. He was relieved to find that the boy spoke English, for he had forgotten the possibility of their having no common tongue.

" I am Prince Anatole Paleologue," said the boy. He spoke proudly, though his teeth were beginning to chatter. " And you ? "

Bill confessed his name. " I've come to help you, if you want me to," he said.

This was different from his expectation, for

he had thought to find the Prince either in a
dungeon or in some place like the House of
Lords, whereas he apparently abode on the
roof-tops like a bird.

" I say, how do you know English ? " was
his next question.

" I was at school in England until a year ago.
Marvell's."

" Well, I'm blowed ! " Peter was going to
Marvell's next year, and half Bill's friends had
been there.

" May I ask you a question ? " said the boy.
He spoke slowly and a little primly, as if
drawing up his English from a deep well.
" How in the name of the blessed angels did
you get here ? "

" Well, you see," said Bill, " I can't quite
tell you, for I don't know. It's magic—quite
good magic. But the point is that I *am* here,
and I've come to help you. Do you mind
telling me—do you usually live on this roof ? "

In the glow of the torch the boy's face showed
a wan smile.

" I came here because I was pursued. I am
in danger. This is my sanctuary, which I have
found for myself. The road to it is difficult,
for you must climb out of the second library
window and reach for a rain-pipe, and then you

climb the pipe, which is not easy if the wind blows."

" Golly ! " said Bill. " That's a job I don't think I would take on. Who's after you ? "

The boy shuddered.

" I don't know . . . I have been here for so many months and only twice I have been allowed outside the gates. That is why I found the way to the roof, for I was tired of being indoors. I have climbed over the whole castle, but no one knows it. It was not easy, for they watch me as if I were a bag of gold. . . . To-night before my supper. . . . I will tell you all—old Mother Linda brings me my supper—she is the only kind face here, for she was my nurse when I was little. To-night Mother Linda did not come, but instead there was a terrible row on the grand staircase. I ran out and saw the sentries struggling with strange men, rough men like peasants from the mountains. I thought it was my friends come to rescue me, but as I looked I changed my mind. For I saw that the sentries, after making much noise, let themselves be overcome and bound, and that all the time they were laughing and joking with their assailants. So I saw that somewhere there was dirty work, and I ran to hide myself. One man saw me and followed, but I was too quick. I dodged through the armoury and slammed the big library door behind me. That door is stiff and hard to open, so I had time to get out of the window. . . ."

Bill wrinkled his brow.

" I expect that was Kuno's doing."

" What do you know about Kuno ? " the boy asked in a startled voice.

" I have heard about him. The papers said that he was the man who was keeping you here. I tell you what—he wants to kidnap you and pretend that you are lost—or perhaps dead."

" That is what I think," said the boy in a small, sad voice. " Here in this castle of Mamizan I am within forty miles of my grandfather. Some day I hope that my friends will release me. But if I were deep among the hills, then I should be buried as if I were in a grave, and my friends would despair."

" You are jolly well not going to be kidnapped," said Bill. " Cheer up, Anatole. . . . But if we sit here much longer we'll freeze. I tell you what—I feel jolly hungry, and you say you've had no supper. What about getting something to eat ? "

" I am horribly empty," said the boy, " but if I go back into the castle I will be captured.

And besides, Mother Linda will be too scared to think of supper."

"There are other places besides this castle," said Bill. "What's a good place for food? Anywhere you like—I don't mind how far it is."

"My grandfather's palace in Grachovo is full of good things," said Prince Anatole.

"Yes, but we can't go there and just ask for dinner. Suppose you were living in the palace and were hungry and didn't want to make a fuss, what would you do?"

"There is the larder," said the boy. "It is as big as a church and full of hams and sausages and pies. And there is the still-room next door, where there will be tarts of many fruits, and spiced bread, and jams and sweet cakes."

"That's the place for us," said Bill. "What is the exact address? 'The Larder, The Palace, Grachovo'—is that how you pronounce it? Now look here, Anatole. You put your arm round my waist, and when I say ' Go ' hold tight. We're going out to supper."

But at that moment a sound fell on their ears which was not the wind. It was the sound of something heavy stumbling in the gutter. The two boys crowded together, and Bill turned off his torch. The noise grew louder. As it chanced, a thin moon at the moment came from behind a bank of clouds, and they saw a man's figure silhouetted against the wild sky.

Bill was enjoying himself. One of the pursuers had found the track of the boy at the library window and had discovered the road by the rain-pipe. He must be a bold fellow to have undertaken the climb, for he was very big and heavy. Bill flicked on the torch and flashed it on him, and a creature was revealed as shaggy as a bear, with naked feet, and wearing a sheepskin coat with the fleece outside. He cried out in triumph and took a long stride towards the boys.

Waving his torch, Bill scrambled to his feet and yelled like a banshee. The man stopped in his tracks, for he saw two boys where he had only expected one. Bill saw his face pale and his hand go to his breast to cross himself.

Then the Prince took a hand. What he cried out Bill did not know, for it was in a strange tongue, but it sounded awful, and the man took a step backward. Clearly the Prince was desperate, for he must have believed that capture was imminent, since he had no knowledge of Bill's magic powers.

" Let us attack him," the boy screamed. " We can fling him from the battlements." And indeed the pursuer seemed to be in such a state of panic that an attack might have succeeded.

"No we don't," said Bill. "Let's go to supper. Hold tight, will you?"

He twisted the stick, and the man of the mountains, shaken by finding two yelling maniacs instead of one frightened child, was now bereft of his senses by the sudden disappearance of the whole outfit. He tumbled on to his face in a swoon of terror.

CHAPTER FIFTEEN

THE ADVENTURE OF THE ROYAL LARDER

HALF an hour later the two boys were sitting on a great cask of beer, placed endways on the floor of a place which seemed half a church crypt and half a corner in the Army and Navy Stores. They had arrived at the larder in black darkness which was made comfortable by the smell of bins and boxes, and sides of dead animals, and great hams in wicker cases. The air was icy cold, but hunger made them forget it, and they fossicked about until on a shelf they found what was clearly the remains of the royal dinner. It had been an ample dinner, for there were several roast partridges untouched, and a pie with only one wedge cut out of it, and the better part of a salmon.

The boys had no plates or knives or forks or spoons, but each had a competent pocket-knife, and with the help of these they proceeded to make a messy but satisfying meal. They had nothing in the nature of bread, so Anatole suggested a visit to the still-room. The door proved to be locked, and the magic staff had to be called into use. Anatole behaved wonderfully well about the staff, for he accepted its ministrations and asked no questions.

" We are better here," he observed, " for we cannot be surprised."

That still-room was full of treasures, and presently they had to desist with regret from their feast, for they could eat no more. There were cakes of every kind, including a confection somewhere between shortbread and almond cake, which fairly ravished Bill's soul. There were tall crystal jars of jam, which they spread thick on sponge-cake, and there were small crisp sugar biscuits, with which Bill filled his pockets in case of emergencies. Lastly they discovered a nest of bottles of bright-coloured syrups, with which they washed down their meal. One tasted of aniseed and burned their throats, but it sent a pleasant glow through their bodies. When they had finished and had perched themselves on the beer barrel they were content and confident once more, and Anatole's thin face had some colour in it.

Bill looked at his watch, and saw that it was

half-past ten, well after the hour when he should have been in bed.

" Now for the next step," he said. " I suppose I should be getting you back to Mamizan."

The Prince shivered. " I suppose so. But oh ! I hate it . . . and I am afraid. Perhaps the mountain men will still be there. . . ."

" Perhaps they will. I tell you what. I'd better go first and prospect. D'you mind staying here until I come back ? I'll leave you my torch—no, I had better take it with me, for I may need it. What's a safe place to land at in that castle—I mean a place where I can find out what is going on and not be spotted ? You see, I don't know my way about."

Anatole thought for a moment. " The best place is the alcove at the head of the grand staircase where the statues are. It is quite dark, but you can see down into the hall, and you are next door to the library and the council chamber."

" Right ! I'm off. I'll be back in ten minutes." Bill twirled the stick and disappeared.

He found himself in an alcove which was shadowy, but not dark. There were heavy curtains across its entrance, but through them appeared the glow of a great illumination. He peeped out and found himself looking at a broad landing from which a wide staircase descended. The place blazed with lights, and from below came the unsteady flare of torches. At the top of the stairway stood an old woman with her back towards him.

She was a tall old woman with a thing like a little black tea-tray on the top of her silver hair, and she was very, very angry. In a voice that suggested thunder and avalanches she was upbraiding the people who stood below. Answers came from them, stumbling, embarrassed answers. Then she turned round, flinging her apron over her head, and Bill could see that she was weeping.

Clearly Mother Linda. It was plain that she was in deep affliction about something or somebody. It must be Prince Anatole, who was believed to have come to grief.

She moved away to the right and Bill could peep farther through the curtains and even dared to venture to the head of the stairs. He saw men below, but they were not of the same type as the monster who had shown himself on the roof. They wore some kind of soldier's uniform, and they appeared to be in a panic, jabbering to each other and every now and then running to what seemed to be the main door of the castle.

The syrup which had tasted of aniseed must have been a potent cordial, for it made Bill's brain very quick. He guessed in a moment what had happened. The kidnappers believed that they had scared the Prince into a flight which had ended in a fall from the roof, and had fled incontinent. The soldiers were now looking for his body among the rocks of the gorge. That was the meaning of the torches.

Bill stole down the staircase until he reached the first angle, whence he could see the hall below. There was no one there, but the great door stood open, and he saw torches flickering in the windy night and heard the confused talk of men. . . . He ventured a little farther and presently was in the hall itself, where the ashes of a fire still smouldered on the cavernous hearth. His object was to get out of doors to see what the soldiers were doing ; but he had not taken two steps across the hall before he pulled up.

Some of them were coming back. There were two—one in the uniform of a common soldier, but the other a smarter fellow wearing a sword. They looked haggard and anxious and their eyes blinked in the bright light of the hall. They saw Bill and stopped, staring, in their tracks.

Then Bill became inspired. He waved his stick and from his lips there came a wail of such blood-curdling poignancy that it almost frightened him. It certainly frightened the two soldiers, for they babbled like men demented and dropped on their knees.

Bill sped up the stairs again and at the top he encountered Mother Linda. He thought that she held out her arms to him, but he had no time to wait, for he realised that he must be off. With another eldritch wail he twirled the stick, and the old woman and the two terror-stricken soldiers found themselves staring into vacancy.

Anatole was still on the beer barrel, but he had sunk into the hollow between it and the wall and was sound asleep.

" You can't go back to Mamizan," Bill told him, when he was fully awakened. " They think you're dead. They took me for your ghost, so I made a bit of a row and I left them praying like billy-o. We have got to decide on your next move. Why can't you stay here ? This is your grandfather's house."

The boy shook his head sadly. " My grandfather is old and weak and cannot protect me. If I were found in the Palace, I would only be sent back to Mamizan."

" Well, haven't you any friends in Grachovo ? The papers said there was a party behind you. You talked yourself about friends. . . ."

The boy exclaimed. " Most certainly I have friends. There is, above all, Prince Zosimo, who is the leader of the loyalists, and who is the cousin of my mother. I will go to him and he will hide me."

Bill had dropped from the barrel and was stamping about with excitement.

" Hide you be blowed ! Don't you see you have got your chance ? Kuno will give out that you have met with an accident and are dead, and that will mean that people will be sorry about you. Then you will suddenly appear, and people will be glad and come over to your side. That is the way things happen in history. It will be a knock-out blow for the republicans, and old Kuno will be in the soup. What is the phrase, ' hoist by his own Packard ' ? "

Anatole followed Bill off the barrel. " That is good counsel. Give your orders, please. We will go to the palace of Prince Zosimo, which is only a quarter of a mile from here. We will go to the Prince's private cabinet."

A stout man with close-cropped grizzled hair was writing at a table. He was in dressing-gown and pyjamas, for he had been about to go to bed, but had remembered a letter which should be written at once. He lifted his eyes from the paper and saw before him two strangely dressed boys. One of the boys carried in his hand a walking-stick.

Prince Zosimo was a man of action. He took two steps and locked the door; then he folded Prince Anatole to his breast.

"We will speak English," said Anatole a minute later, "which His Excellency completely understands. Do not ask me how I have escaped, for that must still be a secret. This is my English friend who has helped me. For the present call him Beel. Now I will tell you the events of this night."

Anatole told the story well, and Prince Zosimo listened in growing excitement.

"It is miraculous," he cried. "I will not ask questions, but how, by all the holy saints, you contrived to get here from Mamizan in an hour or two I do not comprehend. . . . But let that be. These pigs of republicans are in a cleft stick. They must announce your death, my dear Anatole, and who will believe their tale of an accident? We must work upon the suspicions of the people, who do not approve of the murder of children. . . . Then we must have an epiphany—a resurrection. In six days falls the festival of St. Lampadas, when the King, your grandfather, receives in state the notables of Gracia. That will be the fitting occasion. . . . But let us speak no more of it. I will think—think, and the two of you must go to bed, for you are like wraiths from fatigue. In the morning we will summon our friends and make a plan."

So Bill found himself conducted by a tall man-servant to a room which was as warm as a green-house with hot pipes, and in which two camp-beds stood side by side, each covered with a lambskin quilt. Next door was a bath-room, and on the toilet table was laid out a selection from Prince Zosimo's brushes.

" I must be off home," said Bill, when the servant had gone. " Rumple my bed as if I had slept in it, and do not let yourself be called before nine o'clock. I'll be back by then. Good night, Anatole. Sleep sound."

It was half an hour after midnight when Bill crawled between the sheets in his lonely bed-room at Farover. He felt hungry, so he finished the sugar biscuits from the Grachovo larder with which he had filled his pockets.

CHAPTER SIXTEEN

THE SECOND ADVENTURE OF MAMIZAN

BILL did not wake up until half-past eight, and even then Backus, the butler, had to shake him. After that things went badly. His grandmother summoned him to her presence, and he had to listen for twenty minutes to her enquiries about his family. Backus was slow in getting his breakfast, and the sandwiches which he asked for, announcing that he proposed to go for a long walk and not be home until tea, were slow in appearing. Also, he had to write to his mother, as he had promised, and penmanship for Bill was a lengthy business. Happily the weather was fine, inclining to frost, so his day's plans were accepted as reasonable. But it was nearly half-past ten before, in a corner of the shrubbery, he twirled the staff.

He had asked to be taken to the bedroom in Prince Zosimo's palace. The room was empty, his bed-clothes had been rumpled according to his instructions, but there was no sign of

Anatole. Outside the air seemed to be dark with snow-flakes.

Bill thought that he remembered the way to Prince Zosimo's cabinet, but he was wrong. Very soon he was lost in a labyrinth of passages, and when he found a stair it was only a side one, and took him into the back parts of the house. He stumbled upon a knot of servants who were gossiping on a landing, and his arrival produced a sensation. They surrounded him and questioned him in a tongue which he could not comprehend, and all he could do was to utter the word " Anatole " in the way in which Prince Zosimo had pronounced it the night before. The servants looked scared and nervous, and he could not make them understand him. But the situation was saved by the appearance of the footman who had first conducted him to his bedroom. He had clearly had his orders, for he said something peremptory to the others, bowed to Bill, and beckoned him to follow.

He led him through further labyrinths until they reached the main staircase, where Bill recognised his whereabouts. There seemed to be a great many servants about, stationed at every corner, and he observed that they were all armed. " Queer people, the Grachs ! " he reflected. " They let the Prince be shut up in a castle by his enemies and do nothing, but when they get him again they guard him like the Bank of England." The footman stopped at the door of the private cabinet, knocked and entered, while Bill remained outside. When he returned he opened the door for Bill, making another low bow.

There were seven people in the room besides Prince Zosimo and Anatole. Anatole was sitting in a big chair of state, and his feet did not quite reach the ground, while the Prince was at his desk with papers before him. The others were mostly elderly men with pleasant faces, and one must have been a soldier, for he had a great scar on his forehead. There was only one young man, who looked rather like Uncle Bob, his skin was so bountifully sunburnt.

A stool was provided next to Anatole, where Bill very self-consciously sat himself. Prince Zosimo had raised his eyebrows at his appearance and shaken his head, but he did not look cross.

For what seemed hours Bill sat on that stool, till his legs cramped. The men talked in their own tongue and he could not understand one word. It was a funny discussion, for everyone seemed to speak at once, and they shrugged their shoulders and spread out their hands and sometimes rose to their feet in their excitement. Now and then Prince Zosimo would call for silence and say a few words very slowly and solemnly. Anatole did not speak at all.

Suddenly the conversation passed into French, and everybody spoke in low tones, with sidelong glances at the door. Bill did not understand much of that either, but now and then he picked up a word. They all seemed to be talking about " *bouleversements* " and " *degringolades* " and " *émeutes*," and the phrase " *coup d'état* " often cropped up.

Then they began to steal away, one by one. They looked at the windows, outside which the snow was falling thick, and the weather seemed to give them comfort. Bill guessed they were anxious that their presence there should not be known, and that they counted on the snowfall to protect them. Prince Zosimo went out with the last man, and as he passed Bill he smiled and patted him on the shoulder. The two boys were left alone.

Anatole tumbled off the big chair and seized Bill's hand. He was rather pale, but his eyes were glowing.

" I thought you had failed me," he said. " Why were you so late ? What happened ? "

Bill explained the cause of his detention at

Farover. "I'm most awfully sorry I was late. Prince Zosimo isn't suspicious?"

"He is very suspicious, but I have told him that I cannot answer questions yet awhile. This morning I had to tell many lies. I said that you were weary and must not be disturbed, and I would let no one into the room. I waited until ten o'clock before I obeyed my cousin's summons—he was almost angry, I think—and I have not yet had breakfast. Presently there will be *déjeuner*. I have told him that your health is delicate and that you are still weary. But I beg of you, dear Beel, to tell me of yourself and how you came here."

So Bill told him the whole story of the magic staff. Anatole accepted it simply. "It is a gift of God," he said, "sent to make you the saviour of Gracia. But it would be well that Prince Zosimo should not know it, for old men are unbelieving."

"It's your turn to tell me what these men were talking about."

Anatole laughed. "It appears that I am dead. The papers are full of it. I fell last night from a high window at Mamizan. The press of our own party has black borders to-day. My body, when it is found, will be brought to Grachovo and buried in the royal chapel in the

Cathedral. I do not know what they will put in the coffin. A dog perhaps. Kuno always desired for me the death of a dog."

" Will people believe that yarn ? "

" Some will, but not, I think, many. My death is too convenient for friend Kuno's plans. My people will busy themselves in sowing the seeds of suspicion. They will spread ugly stories, and in Parliament Kuno will be asked many questions. Presently most people will believe him a murderer. . . . But there is more than that. It seems that I was to be kidnapped and hidden in the mountains, and that this very week there was to be a rising in Grachovo, when he would proclaim the republic and force my grandfather to abdicate. My death makes that impossible just yet, and gives us time. He would have hushed up the whole thing, but Mother Linda was beside herself with grief and talked to the peasants, and already the tale runs like wildfire. So we are given a little time to prepare our plans. At the Festival of St. Lampadas I will return to life. . . . And then —we shall see."

The boy spread out his thin hands, just like Prince Zosimo.

Bill was thinking hard. He was beginning to realise the amazing power which the staff gave him if he handled it properly. This boy trusted him, and Bill knew that he must rise to the occasion. He felt himself very old and very powerful, so powerful that he was almost frightened.

At luncheon Prince Zosimo talked to him in beautiful English, and he did his best to conduct himself well. It was rather like school, when you went to breakfast with the Head Beak. He was aware that the Prince was burning to ask him questions, but that Anatole had forbidden it. One piece of news interested him deeply.

" I learn," said the Prince, " that Kuno goes to Mamizan this afternoon in spite of the weather. He intends, no doubt, to inform himself about the situation there and to cover his tracks."

" Can't you have him kidnapped?" Bill asked innocently.

Again the Prince spread out his hands. " Would that we could! But we can command no force which could match his guards. Were he but removed from Grachovo for the next week, our plans would march fast."

The two boys were alone for a moment after the meal.

" I'm off," said Bill. " I'm going to Mamizan to see what Kuno is up to. I can't come back to you to-day, for I have to have tea with my grandmother. I'll be back to-morrow morning, and I'll try to get here by ten. You must say I have gone to bed, and you must keep the key of the door in your pocket. Tell the Prince you insist. Dash it all, Anatole, if you're going to be king some day, you have a right to your own way."

Bill had asked to be taken to the alcove on the grand staircase. This time it was as dark as a tomb, for there were no lights in the hall, and when he peeped out he saw only a great dimness, since the heavy snow was blanketing the windows.

Bill had a long time to wait, and it was very cold. He thought pleasantly of the warm fires at Farover, where he was due in an hour or two. He could not afford to be late, for his grandmother would be alarmed, and he must excite no suspicion in that household. Every now and then he popped out from the alcove to get light by which to consult his watch. It was twenty minutes past three before there was a stir below, and a ringing of the great bell and the sound of loud voices.

Bill had made up his mind as to his course,

but he started out on it with a quaking heart. He stole to the staircase head and looked down on a posse of soldiers, in the midst of whom was a tall man in civilian clothes and a big ulster with a fur collar. He had taken off his fur cap, and revealed a long lean head and a face as sharp as a hawk's. He was giving orders, and Bill waited until he saw him begin to ascend the staircase. Another civilian accompanied him—his secretary, perhaps—a fellow in a frock coat.

Bill went slowly down to meet them, keeping his eyes fixed on Kuno and his stick firm in his right hand. At the sight of him the ascending party halted, and the secretary cried out something. Kuno was staring with eyes which even in the gloom seemed very bright and terrible.

Bill was now only two steps above him. " *Mon Général*," he said and saluted.

The grim figure looked mystified and then suddenly wrathful. He seemed about to lay hands on Bill, but Bill anticipated him. He made himself slip, and in falling clutched with his left hand at the belt of Kuno's ulster. Then he twirled the stick and spoke a word.

That word was St. Kilda.

CHAPTER SEVENTEEN

THE KIDNAPPING OF THE KIDNAPPER

A WIND like a knife cut Bill's cheek, and the next second a whiff of salt spray blew in his face. He was among the shingle of a beach, close to a rough stone jetty, and the Prime Minister of Gracia was grunting beside him like a seal on a skerry.

Bill had read a lot about St. Kilda in the papers—how it had been deserted by its inhabitants and was rarely visited by ships, least of all in the winter time. He also remembered from his excursions in Scottish history that it had been used as a place of exile for undesirable people. He had decided on going there during his meditations in the alcove, but he was a little staggered by the reality now that he had reached it.

For in the fading light of the January afternoon it was the wildest and savagest spot that Bill had ever dreamed of. A grey sky hung lowering over a grey shore and a tumultuous sea. Behind him rose a steep hill, with at its foot what seemed to be a huddle of old stone cottages, but no kindly smoke rose from their chimneys. On both sides cliffs hemmed in the bay, and a sheer conical rock stuck out of the yeasty waters. Sea birds hung in a cloud over the forsaken jetty, and their eldritch cries mingled with the howling of the wind. It was very cold, for a south-easter blew straight into the little harbour, and the breakers thundered on the beach like falling mountains.

There was no time to be lost. He had got the most dangerous man in the Balkans as his sole companion on an island fifty miles from anywhere. Kuno was still grunting and rubbing spindrift from his eyes. He rose to his feet blindly like a sleep-walker, and balanced himself unsteadily against the gale.

Bill stealthily withdrew a few paces behind him. He had better get out of it, he thought, before his victim realised his presence. The sea-gulls were the only safe company for General Kuno, who a minute ago had been the autocrat of a considerable state.

After the Hebridean tempest the library at Farover looked very cosy. Bill had not been a minute there before Backus came in to see to

HE ROSE TO HIS FEET BLINDLY, AND BALANCED HIMSELF
UNSTEADILY AGAINST THE GALE.

p. 158

the fire. He was in a good-humour, for he asked Bill about his day's walk.

"You're taking tea with her ladyship, Master Bill," he said. "You'd better tidy yourself up. I'll be sending up tea in half an hour. . . . Hadn't you better leave that stick of yours in the hall? Her ladyship don't like the rooms cluttered up with outdoor things."

When Backus had gone, Bill sat himself down before the wood fire to warm his chilly hands and collect his wits. Life had been very exciting in the past few hours. . . .

Suddenly he was visited by a great compunction.

Kuno was beyond doubt a villain, but St. Kilda was a pretty severe prison-house for the worst of malefactors. And then he remembered that he had left the wretched Kuno no means of subsistence. His fur-lined ulster was his only protection against the winter blasts. He had no chance of making a fire; he had no hope of food unless he ate shell-fish or was lucky enough to knock a gull on the head, and that would be pretty beastly fare. With a horrid start Bill realised that he had condemned the man to death. In a week the big black-backed gulls would be picking his bones on the shore.

He had been feeling rather pleased with himself, but now he understood that he had made an awful blunder. What was to be done? Nothing, except to go back to St. Kilda and move Kuno to some more habitable spot. The prospect set his heart beating. He was afraid of the man with the bright eyes and the hawk face. To move him he must lay hold of him somehow, but Kuno was just as likely to lay hold of him and strangle him before he could twirl the staff.

Bill went through a bad five minutes before his mind was made up, and it says a good deal for him that he did make it up in the end. His pride helped him. He felt that he was having a hand in great affairs and that he must on no account show the white feather.

The weather of St. Kilda had grown worse and Bill arrived in a stiff blizzard of sleet. That was all to the good, for it concealed him from the man, who was standing with one foot in a bog and one on a boulder, alternately calling down maledictions upon fortune and beating his breast with his mighty hands.

Bill had no notion what to do next. He was on higher ground, about two yards from Kuno, and his first idea was to steal behind him and grip his leg or his ulster-band before he could resist.

But suddenly Kuno turned round and caught sight of him.

There must have been something in his eyes, some quaver of fear, which gave Bill a plan. For he leapt on the top of a big stone, waved his stick, and uttered that eerie wailing which he had practised the day before at Mamizan. The big man seemed to shrink and cower.

Then Bill shouted against the wind in that French of his which was a disgrace to the public-school system. "Regard me!" he cried. "I am the Prince Anatole of Gracia. . . . I am the phantom of him you have murdered. . . . You will remain here—here—for ever. . . ."

Bill's foot slipped and he fell off the stone; but fall also did Kuno. The big man dropped on his knees and bowed his head to the ground as if he feared a blow. His massive shoulders were shaking with some profound emotion.

Bill had no difficulty in getting hold of the band of his ulster. He wished himself in the fir wood on Glenmore, far up the slopes of Stob Ghabhar. . . .

Next moment he was in a different kind of weather. The icy winds had gone and a soft drizzling Scots mist shrouded the familiar glen. Kuno was sprawling on a patch of wet moss, and Bill slipped behind a fir tree.

But with the change of scene the terrors of the Prime Minister seemed to have gone. He saw Bill, decided that he had to deal with flesh and blood, and having always been a man of action he was resolved to grapple with it. Before Bill understood what was happening Kuno, with marvellous agility, had sprung to his feet and had almost clutched his collar.

Bill ran for his life. In and out of the fir boles and the dead roots, among russet bracken and over patches of blaeberries the chase proceeded. Now a man of six foot three in the prime of life is faster than a small boy, and Bill realised with horror that he could not put enough distance between himself and his pursuer to be able to use his staff.

His one hope was his knowledge of the ground. Someone had once told him that if you were pursued by a bear you should run transversely along a hillside, for bears' feet were uncertain on a slope; but that if a bull was after you you should run downhill, since bulls had a precarious balance. He thought that Kuno was liker a bull than a bear, so he catapulted himself down towards the ravine of the burn.

Nevertheless he was nearly caught. The pursuit was not a yard behind him when he reached the lip of the gorge. But the gorge saved him.

He reached it at a spot where Peter and he, the summer before, had prospected an ingenious road to the water's edge. It was a road which a boy could take, but not a heavy man. Bill slithered through a patch of dead foxgloves, caught at the root of a birch, and swung himself on to a ledge of rock. Then he slipped down the channel of a tributary rivulet, and landed on a boulder from which he could traverse under an out-jutting crag. The misty weather helped him, and when he reached the edge of the big pool where Peter had caught his first trout he could hear his adversary cursing far above him on the edge of the ravine.

" That was a close shave," thought Bill. " He'll be right enough there. He can stay out all night—serve him jolly well right, too ! And in the morning he will see Jock Rorison's cottage."

About twenty minutes later Bill, having changed his clothes, washed his face and hands, and brushed his unruly hair, sat quietly eating muffins in his grandmother's sitting-room.

"What a lovely colour you have got, Bill dear," she said. "You have been out walking since breakfast, I hear. Did you get far?"

"A good bit," said Bill abstractedly. "Yes, I've covered a pretty fair amount of country to-day."

CHAPTER EIGHTEEN

THE ADVENTURE OF GRACHOVO

THAT evening Bill developed a heavy cold. He thought it was due to the heat of his grandmother's sitting-room after the St. Kilda blizzards. But Backus put it down to his coming back in damp clothes. " I can't think what you was up to, getting so wet, Master Bill," he grumbled. " You comes home nice and dry, and goes out again and gets as wet as a spaniel-dog, and there hasn't been a drop of rain here this blessed day."

Bill snuffled and sneezed at dinner, which he ate in his grandmother's company, and thereafter he was packed off to bed. Grimes, his grandmother's formidable maid, proceeded to doctor him. He was given two extra blankets, had his head wrapped up in a shawl, and was made to drink a beaker of ammoniated quinine. He heard ominous mutterings about a temperature. The result was a troubled night's rest, from which he woke with the snuffles gone but rather limp and miserable. It was his grandmother's orders, conveyed through Grimes, that he should stay that day in bed.

Bill started the day in hope. They were bound to leave him a good deal alone ; he had his stick beside him under the blankets ; and between breakfast and luncheon, or between luncheon and tea, when he was assumed to be asleep, he might slip off to Grachovo. But he was never left alone. Even when he was bidden go to sleep after luncheon, Grimes, who had a mania for doctoring, would tiptoe in every ten minutes to have a look at him.

He had a miserable day. He felt perfectly well, but as restless as a hound tied up in a kennel within hearing of the hunting-horn. In the morning he tried to read old volumes of *Punch*, but in the afternoon, when he was tucked up to sleep, his mind revolved in an unhappy wheel. He felt himself the arbiter of the destinies of Gracia, and yet powerless. What was happening in Grachovo now that Kuno was out of action ? How would Anatole contrive to explain his absence ? He had left Anatole in the lurch—a thought which made him hurl the blankets from him. He liked that little chap better than any boy he had ever met, and he was now separated from him at the crisis of his fortunes.

He slept a bit after tea, and Grimes was so pleased with his recovery that, when she brought in his dinner of soup and minced chicken, she announced that he would be allowed to get up next day.

At half-past eight she put out the lights and left him for the night. Ten minutes later Bill arose and donned all the clothes he could find, including his winter dressing-gown, for his overcoat was downstairs in the cloak-room. Then, having made sure that the house was quiet and that no one was likely to visit him till the morning, he twirled the staff and desired to be taken to the bedroom in Prince Zosimo's palace.

The room was dark except for the lamp beside the beds, but the windows were lit brightly by a glare from without. One was open, and through it came the sound of a terrific clamour from the street below. Snow was no longer falling, but it lay on the roof-tops and reflected eerily the illumination which flickered and trembled on the winter sky. At the window, with his neck craned, stood Anatole. He almost fell out when Bill clapped him on the back.

" Beel, dear Beel ! Where have you been ? "

he cried. " I have been all day sick with longing for you."

" I was ill and they kept me in bed. I say, what's the news ? "

" The news ! " cried the boy. " But of the most glorious ! Yesterday Kuno disappeared."

" I know," said Bill. " I pinched him. Just at present he's having a roughish time in the Highlands."

Anatole called upon all the saints.

" It was the manner of his going," he said. " He disappeared in a flash at the summons of my phantom. His attendants were mad with fright, and all of Mamizan fell on its knees. The tale spread, and presently it reached this city. Meantime the people were angry about my murder. The troops whom Kuno's lieutenants called out mutinied and joined the loyal party. . . . This morning the regiments in the main barracks followed. Kuno's ministry resigned, and all day the courts of my grandfather's Palace have been filled with crowds crying evil on Kuno and good fortune to the house of Paleologue. The tale is that the Devil came for Kuno and carried him off, and the Grachs, who are a religious people, are afraid. . . . Prince Zosimo has become dictator by universal demand. He will be Prime Minister in Kuno's place until the elections can be held, and of their result there is no doubt. Gracia has become loyal once more, and once more I am its Crown Prince with the people's love to support me. And Beel, my darling Beel, to you I owe it all."

A deeply embarrassed Bill found himself embraced and kissed on both cheeks. He realised that Anatole was wearing beautiful clothes.

" What about Prince Zosimo ? " he asked. " Has he been asking questions about me."

" Happily, no. My kinsman has had other things to think about. But soon he must be told all, and it will be a solemn secret in our family. This is not the first time that the good God has come to the succour of the Paleologues. . . . Listen. Prince Zosimo has decided that this night the people must be informed that I am alive and safe. Otherwise they will certainly seek out and crucify every Kunoite in the land. Presently it will be announced from the steps of the Parliament House. Then there will be a rush of people hither, and I must go out on the balcony to greet them. You, my friend and saviour, will stand beside me. . . . Hush ! it begins."

Suddenly it seemed as if the whole air were

filled with bells. Every kind of bell from the shrill treble of little churches to the deep base of the great bell of the Cathedral. And as an accompaniment to this tremendous carillon there was a wilder sound—the babble of thousands of human voices, which rose now and then to a shout that drowned all else and seemed to shake the heavens.

Anatole was hopping about the room in his excitement.

" They come ! they come ! " he cried. " Prince Zosimo will warn us when they are here. . . . At the holy festival of St. Lampadas I will stand at my grandfather's side, and Beel, dear Beel, you will stand beside me. I will have you made a Prince of Gracia. I will have you given the Golden Star of St. Lampadas, which is the highest honour in the land. My grandfather is old, and maybe I shall soon sit in his place, with Prince Zosimo as my regent. Then you will be my chief counsellor and the support of my house. You will not forsake me. . . ."

The boy broke off, for from the street below came a clamour like the falling of great waves. At the same moment Prince Zosimo entered the room. He was white with excitement and very grave, and he wore a resplendent uniform. He smiled on Bill and took his hand. " I am glad to see you are recovered. I fear my duties to-day have not permitted me to enquire about your health." Then to Anatole, " Come, my Prince. The moment has arrived to present you to your people."

Bill's head, what between the dregs of the cold and the excitement of the occasion, was humming like a top. He hardly heard Anatole whisper as he descended the stairs, " To-night I take up my quarters in the royal Palace. When you come again you will find me in the Crown Prince's apartments."

In a daze he entered a huge chamber where many men in uniform were congregated and the windows of which were bright as day from the glow without. He stumbled on to the balcony holding Anatole's hand.

Then came a supreme moment of Bill's life. The three stood behind a low stone parapet— Prince Zosimo superb in uniform, Anatole in a suit of dark velvet, and he himself in a shabby old dressing-gown with a scarf of his house colours round his neck. He looked down upon an ocean of faces, white in the glow of arc lights, and a myriad waving hands and banners. Soldiers lined the street, and, dense as the throng was, there was no disorder.

Every soul there seemed to have a grave purpose.

Anatole stepped forward and held out his hands with a childlike pleading gesture. He, too, was very white, but he was smiling. There was a quiver of a new brightness, as every soldier drew his sword and raised it to the salute. And from the crowd came a cry of welcome which was so passionate and fierce that it seemed to beat like a mighty wind on their faces. Bill remembered a line of a poem which he had had to learn for repetition—

" Sounds, as if some great city were one voice
Around a king returning from the wars."

It was more than he could endure. Another second and he would be howling like a dog and making a spectacle of himself before foreigners. He took a step backward into the shadow, twirled the staff and wished himself in bed.

CHAPTER NINETEEN

THE RESTORATION OF PRINCE ANATOLE

BILL had a fresh dose of cold next morning, which was perhaps not to be wondered at. Grimes was severe with him and kept him tight in bed, threatening to send for the doctor if he were not better in the evening.

For once Bill was content to lie still. The events of the night before had been so overwhelming that he wanted to think them over. Besides, he must get rid of his cold, for in three days fell the festival of St. Lampadas, which was to be the great occasion of his life.

So he lay very peaceful all day in bed, and did not even attempt to read the picture papers which Backus brought him. He lived again in memory through every detail of his adventures in Gracia. The pale little boy he had found on the roof of Mamizan had been very different from the composed young prince who had bowed to the people from Prince Zosimo's balcony. And it had all been his doing. He, Bill, had become a king-maker. I am afraid that he almost forgot about the staff, and was inclined to think too much of his own cleverness.

The thought of Kuno wandering about Glenmore made him chuckle, so that Backus, entering the room with some hot milk, thought he had choked and beat him on the back. Whatever happened, Kuno was out of action. Even if he had time to get back to Gracia before the day of St. Lampadas, it would only be to find himself in imminent danger of lynching. For Kuno Bill cherished a hearty dislike, and he hoped that he would somehow come to fisticuffs with Angus, the river gillie, who was a good man of his hands.

In the evening he was so well that he wanted to get up for dinner, but this was sternly vetoed. It appeared that Grimes had telephoned to his mother and had strict orders to keep him in bed. There was other news from home. It was proposed that he should join Barbara and Peter in their visit to Aunt Alice in London before going back to school. That would mean leaving Farover next day, and his mother suggested fetching him in the car.

The future suddenly became rather complicated, but there was one comfort. Aunt Alice had always allowed him to go off on his own errands, since she believed in letting boys find their feet. Alone he had in the past sniffed around bird-fanciers' shops in Soho, and spent hours in the Natural History Museum. He would find a chance of attending the ceremony of St. Lampadas. But first he must see Anatole and get to know the plans for it.

Next morning even Grimes pronounced him wholly recovered. She brought the news that his mother would arrive at eleven o'clock and carry him home for luncheon. That meant that his visit to Grachovo must be postponed until the afternoon or evening ; but there should be no difficulty about it, for home in the absence of Peter and Barbara would offer many opportunities of retirement. So he spent an hour in his grandmother's room and conducted himself so admirably that he was presented with two pounds, just double his ordinary tip from that quarter.

His mother, when she arrived, made a searching inquisition into his state of health. She observed that he looked thin and a little tired, and was inclined to regret the London plan. But Bill was reassuring. He had never felt so well, he said, and he wanted to see Peter and Barbara and Aunt Alice, and there were many things he would like to do in town. His grand-mother reported highly on his behaviour, and Bill left Farover with an aureole of virtue about his small head.

In the car, on the way back, his mother told him about Uncle Bob's visit. She repeated the story of his miraculous rescue by the French soldiers, about which Bill tried to show an excitement which he could scarcely feel.

" He was very sorry to miss you, Bill dear," she said. " He is tremendously interested in you and asked all kinds of questions. He seemed to be rather anxious about you—I don't know why. He wanted to know if you were quite all right—he asked that again and again until I grew rather worried."

Then she told him the family news. Peter had got his long-promised camera, and Barbara had been to a ball and three plays.

" One afternoon I am going to take Peter and you to a conjuring show at the Albemarle Hall. Won't that be fun ? You always love conjurors."

At luncheon his father had more exciting news.

" I don't know what has come over Glenmore these days," he said. " First there was Mrs. Macrae's delusion before Christmas about the boys. She hasn't got over that yet. She keeps sending me postcards wanting to be reassured about them. . . . And now an extraordinary thing has happened. Three days ago Hector found a queer-looking fellow wandering about the foot of. Stob Ghabhar when he went out in the morning to shoot hinds. He was a big chap, very well dressed, a foreigner who could not speak a word of English, and he was in a furious temper. Hector said that if he had not had his rifle he believed he would have attacked him. Apparently he had been out all night, and he badly wanted food, so Hector took him to breakfast at Angus's cottage. He says he ate like a wolf and then made a long speech in an unknown language, and when no one understood him grew so violent that the two men had to lock him up and send for the police from Abercailly. He was taken off to the Abercailly gaol, and now this morning I have a wire from Stormont, the Chief Constable. It seems that the fellow talks French and says he is a great swell in some foreign country—a general or something—but he doesn't appear to have any notion how he got to Glenmore. I told Stormont to consult Lanerick, who was in the Diplomatic Service and might be able to find out the truth about the man. . . . Fancy a foreign grandee wandering about Stob Ghabhar in mid-winter ! "

It was easy enough for Bill to slip off in the afternoon to a corner of the park and to transport himself to Gracia. He asked to be taken to the Crown Prince's apartments in the royal Palace, and found himself in a magnificence of which he had never dreamed—resembling, he thought, a wonderful restaurant in London where he had once had a meal. By a lucky chance Anatole was there, and the boys curled up on a great sofa and had an hour of excited talk.

Prince Zosimo was too busy, it appeared, to ask questions about the English stranger, and now he, Anatole, was Crown Prince of Gracia and responsible to no one. Things were moving miraculously. The Kuno faction had melted like snow in thaw, and the true desires of the Grach nation were now apparent. Such loyal jubilations Grachovo had never witnessed, and the country was, if possible, more enthusiastic than the capital. A telegram had come from Kuno from Scotland, " I live. I return." But people had only laughed, for there were no Kunoites left except a few hidden in holes and corners.

And then he expounded what would happen on St. Lampadas' Day. The King, his grandfather, now better in health, would drive in the royal coach to the Cathedral, Anatole by his side, and there would replenish with oil the sacred lamp which never went out, and offer gifts on the altar. Then he would return in state to the Palace, where, in the great Hall of Audience he would receive the leaders of the nation and speak through them to all Gracia.

The Prince almost danced with excitement.

" At every step I will be by his side. He will present me to the nobles and they will swear fealty with uplifted swords. I shall wear the ancient dress of Gracia, which is worn only on high occasions of state, and likewise the collar of St. Lampadas. Six of the greatest nobles will attend me, but you, Beel, will be by my right hand, as my principal equerry, and you shall wear on your breast the Gold Star of St. Lampadas, which is given only to those of the highest rank, or to those who have done some great service to Gracia."

" I haven't much in the way of kit," said Bill. He reflected that his best suit would look rather shabby amid such magnificence.

The Prince seized his hand. " Have no fear. You are of my size, and fitting clothes have been ordered for you. They will be of white satin, with a mantle of purple velvet and a belt of mountain turquoises, for that is the historic garb of the Crown Prince's suite on gala days. You shall wear, too, the curved sword of a Gracian noble."

Then he gave Bill explicit instructions. He was to be in his suite in the Palace at eleven o'clock, since at noon the procession started for the Cathedral. Orders would be issued with respect to him, and he would be gazetted to the Prince's staff. Thereafter—Anatole expanded in happy dreams—his dearest friend and deliverer must not leave him. Between them, with the help of the magic staff, they would make Gracia the most prosperous and the most peaceful and the happiest of lands.

He leaped up and kissed him, and somehow this time Bill did not feel ashamed.

That night at dinner his father talked of Bill's future. In these hard times everyone must earn his living, and various careers were passed in review—the Army, the Colonial service, Uncle Bob's family business. Bill listened with apparent attention, but his mind was far away.

He was long in getting to sleep. His father had talked about professions, and had said that you must begin humbly and work your way up. But if he wanted he could be a prince of Gracia, the chief friend of the heir to the throne, and in a year or two, perhaps, the chief friend of the King. The day after to-morrow he would be wearing wonderful clothes and moving among exultant crowds, while soldiers saluted and bands played and cannons boomed. Bill saw the prospect as a mixture of all the high occasions he had ever witnessed—the King's opening of Parliament, the scene at Lords after an unexpected school victory, service in the College Chapel, Speech Day, the Scots Guards pipers, the changing of the guard at St. James's. . . . He hugged himself in his excitement and finally fell asleep with the magic staff firmly clutched in his hand.

CHAPTER TWENTY

THE CROWNING ADVENTURE—I

NEXT morning before going to London Bill looked at the newspapers. He had not done this before, for he had forgotten that what so enthralled him might also interest the world. The papers were full of the doings in Grachovo. There were two or three columns on the foreign page of *The Times*, and *The Daily Mail* had many photographs, including one of Prince Anatole, and a caricature of Kuno.

He could find no word of Kuno's doings. The man was apparently too proud to reveal himself to the police of a foreign country, though he had telegraphed to Grachovo. By this time he must know that his immediate game was up, but he was not the kind of man to despair. He would return to Gracia, and Bill and Anatole and Prince Zosimo would have to keep a sharp eye on his future doings.

On the way to London, as the car passed through the little towns, he saw on all the newspaper placards: " *Scenes in Grachovo* "—

"*Restoration of the Crown Prince*"—"*Defeat of Republican Plot.*" What would the papers say about the ceremony of to-morrow? Bill hugged his staff and had a sudden delicious sense of secret power.

During the journey he was in a happy dream. At luncheon he woke up and was so urbane that Aunt Alice seemed prepared to revise her views about the public school system. Peter babbled happily about his camera and his doings in town. Barbara was not present at the meal, for she was lunching with a friend.

In the afternoon Bill went off by himself, for he had much to do. He wanted to make Anatole a present, for to-morrow's occasion demanded a gift, and he had decided what it should be. His father possessed a sporting rifle, a ·320 which had long seemed to Bill a most desirable possession. If he could provide Anatole with such a weapon his happiness would be complete.

The trouble was that he only possessed in cash £3 10*s*., and he knew that a rifle cost far more than that. Casting about for ways and means, he remembered the five gold coins he had found in the Ivory Valley. They must be valuable, and by their sale he might amass the necessary sum.

So he made for Pratt's in Piccadilly, into whose medal-filled windows he had often stared. He had heard his father say that Pratt's were good people to deal with.

The assistant was courteous and friendly. He looked at the coins, and then summoned a colleague, and the two proceeded to rub and clean them, and to peer at them through magnifying glasses. He asked Bill where he got them, and was told truthfully that they had been found in Africa.

" You have permission to sell them ? " he enquired.

Bill replied with conviction that they were his very own.

They were a long while considering them. They asked for time to consult certain experts, and proposed that Bill should return two days hence.

" But I want to sell them now," said Bill. " You see, I want to give a birthday present to a great friend, and he ought to have it to-morrow."

His eagerness was so great and his candour so engaging that a very serious-looking old gentleman in spectacles, who had been brought into the conclave, was impressed.

" We could make you a price now," he said.

" But I ought to warn you that it may not be a fair price. When we have satisfied ourselves on certain points we might be able to offer considerably more. What do you say to that ? "

" I want to sell them now," said Bill. " How much can you give me ? "

" I'm afraid we can't go beyond twenty-five pounds."

" All right ! I will take that." The sum seemed to Bill an incredible fortune.

He had to give his name and address and sign a receipt, the terms of which were carefully explained to him. Then with a wad of notes in his pocket he sought a famous gunshop in Bond Street. He had once been there with his father and considered it the most delectable place in the world.

The price of the rifle proved to be thirty guineas, just a little beyond his means. Bill was in such despair that the manager was moved. He asked him his name and recognised him as the son of an old customer.

" I'll tell you what we can do," he said. " I have a rifle here which has been returned because the gentleman died suddenly. It is quite new and has never been used, I believe, but you may say it ranks as second-hand. I can let you have it for twenty-five pounds."

So Bill became the possessor of the ·320, and had still a little money left. He arranged that he would call for it next morning at ten.

Bill was restless all evening, and went early to bed, for his mother and Barbara were dining out. He lay awake for a long time, dreaming of the events of the morrow and thinking a good deal about the rifle. Anatole would love it. Anatole was doing a lot for him, but then he had done a lot for Anatole. There were moments when he felt so proud that he could scarcely lie in bed.

The result was that he was late for breakfast, and had to dress in a great hurry. Usually he hated wearing his best clothes, which he was compelled to do in London. But now he only wished that they were better. Never mind ! In an hour or two they would be exchanged for silks and satins.

He had already got his mother's permission to go out for the day, permission the more readily given since Peter was to spend the morning with the dentist. Bill had always had the habit of " prowls "—a family word—and Aunt Alice had supported him in his plea. " Don't coddle children," she had said. " The sooner they learn to stand on their own feet the better."

So, with many instructions from his mother to eat a digestible luncheon and to be careful in crossing the streets, Bill set out from Portland Place clutching his stick.

He took a bus to Bond Street and collected the rifle. Then he indulged in a taxi as far as the Marble Arch. He proposed to find a quiet place in Hyde Park from which to make his departure.

It was a clear frosty morning, and the park was very empty. Bill found a spot where nobody was in sight except two small girls and a dog. When they had disappeared round the corner of a copse, he twirled the staff and wished himself in the Crown Prince's apartments in the Palace of Grachovo.

Anatole was not there, as he had promised. There was no one in the room, and it looked curiously untidy, as if the furniture had been violently moved about. Bill was considering his next step when someone entered, and he saw that it was the young footman who was Anatole's valet.

At the sight of Bill the man cried out something and turned and fled.

Bill heard excited voices outside in the corridor. Then the door was flung open and

Prince Zosimo entered at a run. He was a very dishevelled Zosimo. His short grey hair had not been brushed, and he had certainly not shaved. He was dressed in deep black, but his clothes were wrinkled as if he had slept in them. He came down on Bill like a whirlwind.

" Where have you been ? " he cried, and his English was so disordered that Bill could scarcely follow him. " Where have you come from ? Where is the King ? "

" The King ? " Bill stammered.

" The King ! Anatole is now king. His grandfather died yesterday evening. Where is the King of Gracia ? "

" I don't know."

" But you must know," Zosimo almost screamed. " When did you see him last ? "

" The day before yesterday," said Bill, trying to collect his wits. " What has happened ? Oh, tell me ! "

" Happened ! He is lost. He has disappeared in the night. The Palace guard was relaxed owing to his late Majesty's death. His bedroom was all in confusion. There had been a struggle. There is treason abroad. He has been carried off by the enemy."

" Kuno ! " Bill cried.

" Kuno, doubtless. He must have returned, and he must have had his agents inside the Palace. The police are even now investigating. But he ! But the King ! At noon he should proceed to the Cathedral and thereafter receive his nobles in the Hall of Audience. The sacred lamp must be replenished, and if it fails our cause is undone. And you ! You ! What about you ? You must explain yourself, child, for you are a mystery."

All Bill's happy forecasts were shattered. He felt himself destined now to something very different from the glittering pageant he had dreamed of. But it was anxiety for Anatole that consumed him.

" Please don't ask about me. I've no time to tell you. Anatole knows everything. We must find him."

" Find him ! With all Gracia to search ! He may have been taken across the border. The Cathedral ceremony has been postponed until three o'clock, but it must be held this day, and if the King is not found by three o'clock the monarchy falls."

Zosimo's excitement had the effect of calming Bill. " He will be found," he said.

" Do you know where he is hidden ? " he was asked furiously.

" I can find him," said Bill quietly. " Please listen to me, Prince Zosimo, and do not ask questions now."

Bill consulted his shabby watch. " It's a quarter to eleven. If you will give me until midday I promise to have Anatole back in this room. But you must leave me alone, please. You must lock the door and give me the key."

" You are mad," Zosimo cried.

" Perhaps I am. But I brought Anatole from Mamizan to you, and I got Kuno out of the country. If you trust me I will get the King back and shift Kuno where he won't bother you. If I don't, you can hang me or shoot me."

Zosimo did his best to tear his hair.

" I am plagued with demented children," he moaned. " But I will give you till noon."

He rushed to the door and flung the key at Bill. " There, lock yourself in. Till twelve I go to direct the police search, for all Grachovo is being combed, but at twelve I return, and then you must satisfy me or suffer."

" All right," said Bill. " Good luck to you."

He locked the door and laid the key on a table. He realised that he was in for a much graver adventure than any he had hitherto met, but to his surprise he did not feel nervous. He was too miserable about Anatole and too angry with Kuno. He bitterly regretted that he had been so merciful, and had not left the latter on St. Kilda.

He ordered the staff to carry him to Anatole's side—ordered it with a sick heart, for he feared that he might find Anatole dead.

CHAPTER TWENTY-ONE

THE CROWNING ADVENTURE—II

AT first Bill thought that his worst fears were justified. He found himself in a big, dim place, evidently just under the eaves of some building. There was a low dormer window on his left hand with every pane broken, and outside he saw the sun shining on the tides of a river. Within the air was thick with dust and smelt of stale straw and grain. It must be the upper floor of some waterside mill.

On a heap of straw lay a small figure swathed like a mummy. The body was trussed up in sacking, and there was a bandage over the eyes and what looked like a gag in the mouth. The figure was very still, and Bill in terror laid his ear against its breast. Thank God, it still breathed.

Never had Bill used his stalking knife—a gift last birthday from his father—to more purpose. He slit the sacking and cut the cords, after first removing the gag and the face bandage. Anatole was revealed clad in pale-blue silk pyjamas.

His eyes were open and staring, and at first there was no recognition in them. But he was alive.

Then a sound fell upon Bill's ear, the sound of heavy snoring. There was someone else in the room, someone sleeping in the straw only a few yards away.

He saw that Anatole had now recognised him and was making feeble signs. The signs were for caution and silence. Bill put his head to the boy's lips and heard him murmur " Kuno."

Very slowly Anatole began to move. His limbs were cramped, and his face was twisted with pain as he moved them, but he made no sound. Gently he raised himself until he sat up, and then he clutched Bill's arm, and there was terror in his eyes.

" Oh, Beel," he whispered, " take me away. They are going to murder me. . . ."

" Not they," said Bill. " Hold my arm, Anatole. I can shift you out of here any moment. But we must think. We need not be at the Palace for an hour. Tell me, what happened ? Yes, hold me as tight as you can. You are quite safe. Now very slowly—I am listening. That hog over there won't wake."

The boy had now mastered himself, but he still shivered like a frightened colt.

"Kuno," he whispered. "Yesterday he came back. By air, it must have been. . . . My grandfather died suddenly before dinner. That you have heard. There was confusion in the Palace, for the discipline had become weak—and there was treachery, which, please God, I will yet discover and punish. . . . I went to bed and slept sound, for I was very weary. The next I knew was that I was in the hands of rough men—mountain men, I think. I fought, but I was easily overcome, and I could not cry out, for my head was muffled. Then I think I fainted, for I remember nothing until I came to my senses in this place. I saw Kuno—and others. I heard them talk, for they did not fear me any more, and spoke openly of their plans."

"Where are we now?" Bill asked.

"In Grachovo. By the river side, in a disused warehouse. There are men here they call the Water Rats—secret people who have long defied our police. They are Kuno's instruments. This night I am to be taken down the river away from Grachovo. They spoke of killing me first, but Kuno forbade it. 'Not yet,' he said. But he means to kill me, Beel, and hide my body far from Gracia, so that none will ever know my fate. . . . Oh, take me away! Save me, dear Beel, save me!"

There was an hysterical note in the boy's voice which alarmed Bill. He stroked his head and put his arm round his shoulders.

" You are quite safe. Don't be afraid. But you are the King now, you know, and must look a bit ahead. We can't leave Kuno here."

" We will return with a regiment and surround this place." A wholesome wrath was entering Anatole's voice.

" He might escape. Besides, you don't want a big public row just at present. It would only stir up the Kunoites. Far better shift the brute to some place where he can't get away in a hurry. Our first job is to settle with Kuno."

" But you will not leave me ! " Terror was mounting again.

" Let's both go. He is sleeping pretty sound ? "

" He is very weary. He said that he must have eight hours' sleep, for he flew from somewhere far away."

" All right. Now do exactly as I tell you. Get a firm hold of my braces. We are going on a journey."

Anatole rose staggeringly and balanced himself on his bare feet. Bill kicked off his shoes, his best shoes. They were never seen again, and their loss led to fierce recriminations from Elsie the nurse.

The two boys stole across the room to the heap of straw where sprawled the figure of a sleeping man. Kuno was still in the clothes which Bill had last seen at Glenmore, including the fur-lined overcoat. But someone—perhaps Lanerick, the Lord-Lieutenant of Perthshire—had given him a knitted woollen muffler. To Bill's amusement it was in the colours of his own school. The man lay on his side with his face away from the boys, and his breathing told them that his slumbers were deep.

Bill, as he had done before, grasped the belt of Kuno's greatcoat, while Anatole held on to his braces. Then with his right hand he twisted the staff.

" I want to be taken to a quiet place near Moscow," he said.

It was like tumbling into a cold bath. Bill found himself in what looked like a snow-covered brickfield. It was grey, biting weather, and the place seemed the last word in dreariness, for under the leaden sky the squalid and ruinous houses seemed to stretch endlessly.

Kuno lay on the ground slowly wakening.

The two boys slipped off to a distance of some yards and watched him as he rubbed his eyes and shambled to his feet like a great ox.

" This is the place for him," said Bill. " He will be at home among the Bolshies. . . . Golly ! it's cold. Speak to him, Anatole. Say good-bye nicely."

Anatole, freezing in his silken pyjamas, managed to say a good deal. It was in a tongue which Bill did not understand, but its effect on Kuno was plain enough. Amazement, fear, and fury chased each other across his expressive countenance. The last words of all must have had a special sting, for with a roar the big man started towards them.

" We had better hop it," said Bill. But before he twirled the stick he added to the commination service something on his own account, in the most abusive French he could compass. It was " *Sale bête ! maintenant vous l'avez pris dans le cou.*"

The Palace was beautifully warm, and in his own room the frozen Anatole was himself again. He flung himself on Bill and hugged him, and then skipped about the floor to get the stiffness out of his legs. " I must have a bath," he cried, " and food, for I am famished." Then he caught sight of a long green case on the table. " What is that ? " he cried.

" It's my present to you," said Bill. " I thought you'd like it. It is a sporting rifle just like my father's."

The boys were deep in the examination of its marvels, and Anatole was lying flat on a couch sighting it over a cushion, when the hour of midday boomed from the Cathedral tower and reminded Bill of his duty. He unlocked the door, rang the bell, and summoned a servant.

" His Majesty requires the attendance of Prince Zosimo," was his order.

When Zosimo, still dishevelled and grey with care, presented himself, he was confronted by his King in fluttering pyjamas holding a small rifle at the present.

" Rejoice, my uncle," said Anatole, " for all is well. The great Beel has brought me back, and, as you see, he has armed me. Bid the police cease their activities. The Water Rats we will gather up at our leisure. As for friend Kuno, the good God has him in keeping. At this moment he is perhaps trying to explain to the Soviet officers what he is doing in the suburbs of Moscow. I think the task will not be easy."

Thereafter Bill walked into a romance which was beyond his craziest dream. He was given a bath in hot scented water, and though he cordially disliked all scents he rather enjoyed it. Then came a little man in white linen who begged permission to arrange his hair, and Bill, who did not love barbers, submitted as to a high ceremonial. Then a valet dressed him in the clothes which had been appointed—a jacket and breeches of white satin with gold buttons, white silk stockings, and wonderful white leather shoes with black rosettes, since the Court was in mourning for the dead monarch. Round his waist was clasped a belt of fine gold mesh studded with rough turquoises from the mountains, and from it was suspended the curved sword of a Gracian noble. On his left breast was pinned the gold star of St. Lampadas ; it had five points set with brilliants, and in the centre was the enamelled figure of that saint in his famous act of bearing the lit Lamp of the Temple through what appeared to be a cyclone. From his shoulders hung an embroidered cloak of purple velvet, and on his head was a peaked cap with an osprey's plume set in a jewel of emeralds.

By all his standards he should have felt a fool, for had he not invariably made a scene at home when he was compelled to go to a fancy-dress party? But Bill did not feel a fool. I am afraid he felt rather like a hero. He had his lunch alone, but, though the lunch was excellent, he ate little, thereby obeying one of his mother's injunctions that morning.

The afternoon passed like a dream. The city was in mourning, but also keyed up to a tense excitement. There was no music as they drove in the state coaches to the Cathedral through the packed streets, and indeed little sound of any kind. The people were waiting until the sacred Lamp was replenished and the life of Gracia could begin its new year.

In the great, dim Cathedral Bill stood a little behind the new King, while the organ boomed, and the trebles of the choristers rose with the joy of a spring sunrise. Bill had eyes only for Anatole, as he knelt before the altar and received from the hands of the Archbishop the sacred oil. This boy, only a little older than himself, was taking charge of a nation and dedicating himself to a high purpose. Bill forgot all about himself and the magic staff and honour and glory. He felt shy and solemn and abashed, and full to the brim of good resolutions.

But when they emerged from the Cathedral the pomp of the world again laid hold of him.

For now the people of Grachovo seemed to have done with their mourning, though the old King lay dead in their midst. They hailed a new King and a new world. The national anthem of Gracia rose like a strong wind. The band of the Royal Guards played it and a hundred thousand voices joined in. Never had Bill heard such music. It was like all the bold songs he remembered—" Rule Britannia " and " Blue Bonnets over the Border " and " Men of Harlech "—blended in one superb defiance. He sat up very stiff in the royal carriage and tried not to cry.

But in the Hall of Audience he did cry, for that was more than flesh and blood could bear. There was no King to present the Crown Prince to the nobles, for the Crown Prince was now King and had to present himself. When Anatole stepped forward, very little and quaint in his Field-Marshal's uniform, and in a breaking voice asked for the allegiance of his people, there came a shout which made the walls tremble, and a hundred swords flashed upwards. The King was so small and so young and had come through so much tribulation, that the faces below the dais, many of them grim and scarred, melted into a sudden tenderness. There were tears in the Hall of Audience, a portent which had not been seen for many a day.

Said Prince Zosimo, speaking to himself:

" The monarchy is secure. Nay, Gracia is secure, for she has found an authority which she can love."

An hour later, while Bill was hurrying into his own clothes, Anatole sat by him, pale but happy, and with a strange dignity in his face.

" You will come back soon, dear Beel," he said. " I shall be busy, for now I must rule with the aid of my Regency Council, but without you I shall be a lonely king."

Bill arrived in his bedroom in Portland Place about six o'clock. He waited there until it was time to dress, for he did not want to talk to anybody.

" I never heard you come home," his mother told him, when the family met in the drawing-room before dinner. " Have you had a good day ? "

Bill nodded. " Good " was scarcely the word he would have chosen. He was very quiet all evening, and played draughts with Aunt Alice besides visiting Peter in bed. Something tremendous had happened to him, a destiny with which he could not quite cope.

He had been switched to the top of a high mountain, and he wondered how he was going to take up his road in the valley again. He felt rather old, and yet desperately conscious that he was young and feeble and of no particular account. For the first time in his life Bill knew what it was to be humble.

CHAPTER TWENTY-TWO

THE GOING OF THE STAFF

NEXT morning Bill rose with a cloud on his mind. He had slept long and deep and had had no dreams, but as soon as he opened his eyes he knew that something was amiss. It was a detestable morning, foggy with a slight drizzle, and he dressed in a mood of despondency which he could not understand.

The marvels of yesterday could never happen again. That was the only thing about which he was clear. Something must come between him and Anatole, for how could an ordinary school-boy in England, not much respected by his masters, keep up his friendship with a far-away King? And yet he liked Anatole so much that his eyes filled when he thought of leaving him. And Anatole needed him too. He would be very solitary among the old men. And there was Kuno ramping among the Bolsheviks. Some day Kuno would come back and make trouble.

But he had still the magic staff. That was his only consolation amid his forebodings. He handled it lovingly and it gave him a little comfort.

At breakfast he did not look at the papers. No doubt they were full of yesterday's doings in Grachovo, but he did not want to read them. He preferred to keep his memory select and secret like a dream.

He spent the morning indoors with the now convalescent Peter, making believe to be deeply interested in his new camera. Aunt Alice, after her fashion, announced that he was an odd boy but had clearly a good heart.

In the afternoon came the conjuring show at the Albemarle Hall. In the past Bill had shown an inordinate appetite for such entertainments, but now the idea seemed to him merely silly. What were disappearing donkeys and vanishing ladies compared to the performances which he had lately staged? But he had to pretend to be enthusiastic, feeling that good manners were required from an associate of princes.

When they reached the door of the hall he had an unpleasant shock. He was required to give up his stick and receive a metal check for it. To his mother's surprise he protested loudly. " It won't do any harm," he pleaded. " It will stay beside me under the seat." But the rule was inexorable and he had to surrender it.

" Don't be afraid, darling," his mother told him. " That funny stick of yours won't be lost. The check is a receipt for it, and they are very careful."

The world had darkened for Bill, and all his forebodings of the morning returned. While Peter gurgled and giggled, he spent an hour and a half of black misery. This was worse than last half when the stick had been left behind at home. He kept his eyes tightly shut, for he could not take the slightest interest in the antics on the stage. Happily his mother could not see him ; she thought that his stillness was due to an intense absorption.

When the performance came to an end he dragged his mother and Peter furiously through the crowd ; but they had been near the front of the Hall and were slow in reaching the entrance. With his heart in his mouth he pushed up to the counter. There was no sign of the man who had given him the check. Instead there was a youth who seemed to be new to the business, and who was very clumsy in returning the sticks and umbrellas.

When it came to Bill's turn he was extra slow, and presently announced that he could find no No. 229. Bill was almost in tears. His mother, seeing his distress, intervened, and sent the youth to look again while other people were kept waiting. But the youth came back with the same story. There was no duplicate No. 229 or any article corresponding to Bill's description.

After that he had to be allowed to attend to the others, and Bill waited hysterically until the crowd had gone. Then there was a thorough search, and Bill and his mother and Peter were allowed to go behind the counter.

But no No. 229 could be found, and there were no sticks left, only three umbrellas.

Bill was now patently weeping.

" Never mind, darling," his mother said. " We must go home now, or Aunt Alice will be anxious. I promise that your father will come here to-morrow and clear up the whole business. Never fear—the stick will be found."

But Bill had the awful conviction in his heart that it was lost.

When Bill's father went there next day and cross-examined the wretched youth he extracted a curious story. If the staff was lost, so also was the keeper of the walking-sticks, for the youth was only his assistant. The keeper —his name was Jukes and he lived in Hammersmith—had not been seen since yesterday afternoon during the performance. Mrs. Jukes had come round and made a scene, and that morning the police had been informed.

Mr. Jukes, it appeared, was not a very pleasant character, and he had had too much beer at luncheon. When the audience had all gone in, he had expressed to his assistant his satiety of life.

The youth's testimony ran as follows :

" Mr. Jukes, 'e was wavin' his arm something chronic, and carryin' on about 'ow this was no billet for a man like 'im. He picks up a stick, and I thought he was goin' to 'it me. ' Percy, me lad,' says 'e, ' I'm fed up—fed up to the back teeth.' He starts twirling the stick, and says 'e, ' I wish to 'eaven I was out of 'ere.' After that I must 'ave come over faint, for when I looks again, 'e 'ad 'opped it."

Mr. Jukes's case is still a puzzle to his bereaved wife and to the police, the general idea being that he had levanted to escape the responsibilities of his family. But Bill understands only too clearly what happened. Mr. Jukes

SO IF YOU MEET ANYONE LIKE HIM, LOOK SHARPLY AT HIS BUNDLE,
AND IF IT IS THERE AND HE IS WILLING TO SELL, *BUY, BUY, BUY,*
OR YOU WILL REGRET IT ALL YOUR DAYS.

and the staff have gone " out of 'ere," and where that may be neither Bill nor I can guess.

In the miserable weeks that followed Bill reasoned out the matter with himself and came to this conclusion. The staff was not *Beauty*, but *Bands*, and he attributed his loss to the fact that he had been thinking too much of his own amusement. He did not believe that *Bands* had republican principles and disliked monarchies. But *Bands* had come to dislike *him*. He had been too proud and had thought a great deal about his own cleverness, when it was the staff that did everything. *Bands* wanted to teach him humility, or perhaps *Bands* meant well and understood that Bill had simply got himself into a position where going on was impossible. He had cut in on the road too far ahead, and must now go back and retrace the path from the start.

So Bill wrote to Anatole and told him what had happened, and received in return a letter which made him howl, but which also heartened him. Some day Bill would come to Grachovo, or if he did not Anatole would come to England, for, said the King of Gracia, " We two have gone through so many difficult places that fate cannot separate us."

Bill is very humble nowadays, and at the back of his head he has a faint hope that somehow or other and sometime or other the staff may return to him. He would even be content if he knew that it was back in the ordinary world, though in the possession of someone else, for he cannot bear to think that a thing so wonderful should have gone altogether out of human life.

So he wants me to broadcast this story.

Let every boy and girl keep a sharp eye on shops where sticks are sold. The magic staff is not quite four feet long and about one and a quarter inches thick. It is made of a heavy dark red wood, rather like the West Indian purpleheart. Its handle is in the shape of a crescent with the horns uppermost, made of some white substance which is neither bone nor ivory. If anyone sees such a stick, then Bill will give all his worldly wealth for news of it.

Failing that, he would like information about the man who sold it to him. He is very old, small and wizened, but his eyes are the brightest you ever saw in a human head. He wears a shabby greeny-black overcoat which reaches down to his heels, and a tall greeny-black bowler hat. It is possible that the stick may have returned to him. So if you meet anyone like him, look sharply at his bundle, and if it is there and he is willing to sell, *buy*, *buy*, *buy*, or you will regret it all your days. For this purpose it is wise always to have a farthing in your pocket, for he won't give change.

THE END

If you liked this story then why not look out for other Kelpies. There are dozens of stories to choose from : ghosts, spy stories, animals and the countryside, witches, mysteries and secrets, adventures and many more. Kelpie paperbacks are available from all good bookshops.

For your free Kelpie badge and complete catalogue please send a stamped addressed envelope to:
Margaret Ritchie (K.C.B.),
Canongate Publishing Ltd.,
17 Jeffrey Street, Edinburgh
EH1 1DR.